Books by Tristan Bancks

The Tom Weekly series

My Life and Other Stuff I Made Up

My Life and Other Stuff that Went Wrong

My Life and Other Massive Mistakes

My Life and Other Exploding Chickens
(new edition available June 2018)

My Life and Other Weaponised Muffins
(new edition available June 2018)

My Life and Other Failed Experiments
(yes, Tom Weekly is back with more weird, funny, gross,
BRAND-NEW adventures in July 2018!)

Two Wolves

The Fall

The Mac Slater series

Mac Slater, Coolhunter

Mac Slater, Imaginator

TOM WEEKLY

MY LIFE AND OTHER STUFF THAT WENT WRONG

AS TOLD TO

TRISTAN BANCKS
AND
GUS GORDON

RANDOM HOUSE AUSTRALIA

A Random House book
Published by Penguin Random House Australia Pty Ltd
Level 3, 100 Pacific Highway, North Sydney NSW 2060
www.penguin.com.au

Penguin
Random House
Australia

First published by Random House Australia in 2014
This edition published in 2018

Addresses for the Penguin Random House group of companies can be found
at global.penguinrandomhouse.com/offices.

A catalogue record for this
book is available from the
National Library of Australia

NATIONAL
LIBRARY
OF AUSTRALIA

ISBN: 978 0 14379 009 9

Cover and internal illustrations by Gus Gordon
Cover design by Astred Hicks, designcherry
Internal design by Benjamin Fairclough © Penguin Random House Australia,
based on original series design by Astred Hicks, designcherry
Printed in Australia by Griffin Press, an accredited ISO AS/NZS 14001:2004
Environmental Management System printer

Random House Australia uses papers that are natural, renewable and
recyclable products and made from wood grown in sustainable forests.
The logging and manufacturing processes are expected to conform to the
environmental regulations of the country of origin.

Contents

Hey.

I'm Tom Weekly, and this is my life. I write stuff down and draw pictures to make sense of all the crazy stuff that happens to me. Like when Jack and I started a freak show in the playground, and when Stella Holling tried to kiss me, and when my nan decided she was going to climb Mount Everest.

So here it is . . . my second book of weird, funny, sometimes gross stories. (Whatever you do, don't read the first book. It'll give you dumb ideas that adults will not appreciate. Like eating sixty-seven hot dogs in ten minutes. Or building a teleporter. Or pretending you have appendicitis to get out of detention with your school librarian.) My friend Raph has a story in this book, too. If you want to send me a message or a joke or one of your own weird stories that I could stick in my next book, I'm at: TheTomWeekly@gmail.com

Giddyup.

Tom

Freak

'Roll up! Roll up! He's the most hideous freak you have ever laid eyes on! He's disgusting! He's disgraceful! He will make you vomit!'

'Settle down,' I whisper to Jack through the thin red curtain.

'What?' Jack asks, poking his head inside.

'You don't have to say they'll vomit.'

Jack rolls his eyes and shuts the curtain. 'You will not vomit!' he announces in the same ringmaster voice. He goes on to use words like 'gasp' and 'horror' and, 'This lunchtime only. Just two dollars!'

I am sitting inside a small red teepee that Jack and I have built under the trees at the far end of the bottom playground. The teepee is made of long, straight branches and a red sheet from my house.

Jack thinks this pop-up freak show will make us wealthy beyond our wildest dreams, and I need cash to buy a birthday present for Sasha, something that will convince her to go out with me again. I want to prove to her that I'm not selfish and weird like she says.

'You ready for the first customer?' Jack asks, poking his head back inside.

I look at my socked foot, nervous.

'I guess,' I say.

Jack whips open the curtain and says, 'Welcome! Welcome!'

Brent Bunder appears. He is a giant bulldozer of a kid with diggers for hands. He fills the teepee.

'Take a seat,' I squeak.

Brent Bunder lowers himself awkwardly onto one of the kindergarten chairs we have borrowed. It strains and moans under his weight.

'This better be good,' he grunts. He is red-faced and sweaty, like he just guzzled a bottle of hot chilli sauce. He looks uncomfortable, crammed into the tiny space. I want to run but I can hear Jack outside dropping another coin into his lunch box.

So I slowly peel my limp, grey sock down over my ankle. Over my heel. Down my foot.

Brent watches on as
I close my eyes and
reveal my toes.

My webbed FEET

Silence.

I open one eye.

And there it is.

My foot.

One. Two. Three. Four.

Four toes. Slightly webbed. Like a cartoon
duck. It has been that way since birth. I have
never really shown anyone apart from Jack and
my family. My sister says it is proof that I'm a
mutant from another planet.

Brent Bunder looks on, expressionless.

'There are only four,' I explain helpfully.
Brent Bunder isn't exactly top of our year in
maths.

Still nothing.

'There are meant to be five,' I say.

He pokes my toes with one gigantic finger, like he is checking that they are real, that I haven't bought them from a magic shop.

Eventually he says, 'So what? You're deformed. Is that what I paid two bucks for? Now I can't buy an iceblock, and I'm hot.'

'Well . . .' I say, looking up at him. He does look hot. His face is speckled with tiny beads of sweat.

'I want my money back.'

'Sure. No problem,' I say.

Jack's face appears through the gap in the sheet behind Brent. He shakes his head and mouths the words, 'No way.'

I look at Brent. Angry, sweaty, bulldozer Brent. He could crush me like a can. How can I make this worth two dollars?

'Would you believe a bear bit it off?' I say, half-joking.

'What?'

'Well . . .' My mind whirrs, scanning for ideas. 'When I was little we lived in Canada and . . . I was two years old and playing down by the creek at the back of my house, and this . . . black bear, a big one, came along and . . .'

Brent Bunder looks totally suspicious.

'And he started growling at me, but he was over the other side of the creek. And I crawled away but this grizzly –'

'You said it was a black bear,' Brent says.

'This black bear started swimming across the creek, and when he reached my side he . . . attacked me,' I explain.

'Attacked?'

'Well, he bit me. On the foot. Bit the toe

clean off. My mum heard screaming and she ran down to the creek. When she saw the blood dripping down the bear's chin and the missing toe, she fainted and –'

'Bears have chins?' Brent questions.

'Well, yeah, the furry bit just below their mouth.' Brent leans forward, looking me in the eye. 'And my big sister picked me up and ran two k's to the hospital, and they stitched me up. That's why the toes are sort of webbed. Because of the stitches.'

Brent fixes me with a distant look, like he's replaying parts of the story in his mind. 'What happened to the bear?' he asks.

'Um . . . I d'know. It went off into the forest and . . . maybe it ate some other kid's toe. Maybe it wanted the complete set,' I suggest. 'Y'know. Collect all five!'

WANTED

Toe muncher of
Icky Creek

Goes by the name
of 'Bear'
$10·00 reward for
missing toe

I hold his glare, waiting for him to punch me really hard in the nose or rip the teepee apart in a rage. But, instead, he says, 'You're a freak, mate. I love it.' He stands and turns to go. 'Oh, by the way, I want a third of the profits.'

'Why?'

'Because I'm big and you're small.'

'Fair enough,' I say.

'I'll be back at the end of lunch to collect.' Then he ducks outside. 'It's awesome!' he announces to the other kids. 'You wait till you hear how it happened.'

And that is it. From then on, I am unstoppable. I tell each kid a different story and swear them to secrecy. The tales get taller every time.

'A shark bit it off,' I tell Morgan Brett.

'As if. How?' he asks.

'My dad's a fisherman. For the first two years of my life we lived on a trawler at sea, and one day he netted a shark about a metre-and-a-half, two-metres long.'

'Get out.'

'The shark slipped out of the net and slid across the boat's deck. I was crawling around, playing with my jack-in-the-box, and the shark's mouth came to rest right near my foot.'

my missing toe

His eyes widen. I make a chomping sound and a snapping motion with my hands. Morgan is gobsmacked.

'Next!' Jack shouts.

And so it goes.

I tell Millie Randall my toe was trapped in a piece of machinery.

Another kid, that a flesh-eating disease rotted it off.

Caught in the spokes of a motorbike.

Trampled by a horse's hoof.

Hacked off by a chainsaw.

Lost in a bet.

Jack warns me to pull back on the stories, but I'm on a roll. By the time the last kid leaves the teepee near the end of lunch, we have fifty-eight dollars in cold, hard change. For the first time in his life, Jack was right: we are rich!

I have just started packing up the chairs when Sasha pokes her head into the teepee.

Sasha. The cutest girl in Australia. My ex-girlfriend.

'Hey, Tom,' she says, real sweet. White jumper, hair in a ponytail, eyes like blue sky.

'Hi,' I say.

'What's the freaky thing that everyone's talking about?'

'Nothin'.'

'I want to know. I've paid my money.'

There is no way I can show Sasha my freaky foot.

'Jack, we have to make a refund,' I call out. 'The bell's about to go.'

Jack pokes his head through the curtain next to Sasha. 'It's okay. We still have time.'

'No we don't.'

'Yes we do.'

'Don't.'

'Do.' He mouths the word 'sixty' to me.

Sixty bucks. That's how much we will have if I show Sasha my missing toe. A nice round sixty. Twenty for Jack, twenty for me, twenty for Brent Bunder, the filthy scoundrel. Four weeks' pocket money for one hour's work. Enough to buy Sasha's present.

'Are you going to show me or not?' she asks.

'Just give me a moment,' I say.

I slip out of the teepee to find Jack and Brent waiting for me.

'I am not showing Sasha,' I say.

'Show her or I'm keeping the money,' Jack replies.

'What?'

'It was my idea.'

'It's my foot!'

Brent makes a throat-slitting motion with one of his giant sausage fingers and points towards the teepee.

So I scowl and go inside.

I sit down.

Me and Sasha. And the toe. The missing toe.

'What's so bad?' she asks.

'You'll see.'

I start to peel the sock down.

What should I tell her? The truth? Or one of my stories? I don't want to mess this up. I don't want to ruin my plan of marrying Sasha and having three kids and a Labradoodle and a house overlooking the ocean with secret passages and revolving bookcases.

Over the ankle, over the heel.

Don't do it, I think.

Sasha looks on, fascinated.

Over the foot, over the toes and . . .

There they are in all their freakish glory.

Boom.

Sasha stares. Little creases appear in her forehead.

'How did it happen?' she asks quietly.

Um, I think. I don't want to lie to her but she deserves a good story, a better story than anyone, just for being Sasha. 'I was born like

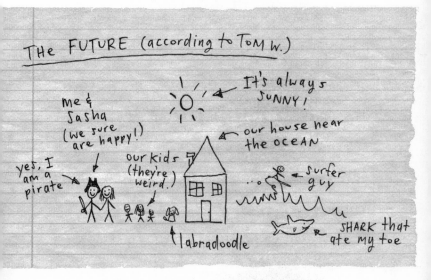

that' just isn't worth two dollars. So I open up my mind and the story seems to fall from the sky.

'When I was four my sister's guinea pig escaped from its hutch,' I say, intense, serious. 'But this was no ordinary guinea pig. It was *twice* the size of a regular one. Feral. I think she found it in the bush. I was in the sandpit playing cars one day and I heard its claws on the concrete path. I turned and saw it coming for me. I backed off into the corner of the pit. I threw a Matchbox car at the beast, but it just raised a paw and batted it away. I screamed but Mum was out front cleaning the car and didn't hear me. It climbed up on the wooden edge of the sandpit and reared up on its back legs, like a wrestler ready to launch himself off the top turnbuckle. I freaked and ran. It chased me across the grass, up the back steps and halfway across the veranda, then it pounced, ripping my toe out of the socket with its razor-sharp teeth. I screamed and clutched my foot as it retreated to its hutch to pick the flesh off the bone and digest its gruesome meal.'

Sasha stares, open-mouthed. I breathe hard. I have given it everything. It is a story

a toe-biting
feRAL
Guinea Pig

worth five bucks, not two. It is a movie, really.
Dreamworks will probably want to buy the
rights. It is the greatest story about a feral
guinea pig ever told.

I look at her.

She smiles. She looks so beautiful it hurts.

'That's a lie,' she says.

'Huh?'

'Tell me what really happened. Were you
just born like that?'

I feel like an idiot. So I say the obvious
thing: 'No. That's what really happened.'

'Tom,' she says, trying to make me smile.
But I won't. I'm in too deep now. I have to see
this through. Otherwise she will think I am a
liar, and she will never marry me, and we will
never own a Labradoodle.

'That's the truth,' I say.

She shakes her head. 'Why would you look me in the eye and lie to me, tell me such a dumb story.'

Dumb! She actually says the word 'dumb'.

'And then you don't even have the guts to admit you made it up.'

'But I didn't!'

Sasha stands. 'Jack was right. You are hideous. Not your toes. Just you.'

'But –'

She vanishes through the curtain. I chase her.

'How'd that go?' Jack asks.

'Yeah. Great,' I say, pushing past him.

'Sasha!' I call, but she's walking off across the playground and out of my life.

'I'm telling everyone you're a liar!' she shouts. 'You'll have to pay every cent back.'

'Wait. Sasha. Please!'

She keeps walking. I've blown it. This is the worst moment of my life, until . . .

I feel a heavy hand on my shoulder. It spins me around.

'I want my money. Now.' It's Brent Bunder. He is not smiling.

'But –'

Jack is standing just behind Brent. Jack pulls the elastic waistband on his track pants forward and pours all the money out of his lunch box and into his undies.

'You . . . idiot!' I say. I can't help it.

Brent turns to Jack, and Jack starts running away with all the money. I twist out of Brent's grip and sprint across the playground – one shoe on, one shoe off. Brent gives chase. I hit the basketball courts, my bare, webbed foot slapping against the tar. I catch up with Jack and we bolt towards the front gate of the school. Jack's underpants are jingling like mad.

'You're scrubbing that money clean,' I snarl at him and look back to see Jonah Flem, Morgan Brett, Millie Randall and Brent Bunder racing after us. And, further back, Sasha, standing with her arms crossed. My classmates, the girl I love and the school's resident giant are after my blood.

'You're dead!' Brent Bunder screams.

So Jack and I keep running – a cheap sideshow freak and a scam artist. As we pick up speed, the coins begin to rain down from Jack's pant legs, leaving a golden trail of lies and broken dreams.

We stop at the gate to catch our breath. Jonah, Morgan, Millie and Brent are grabbing all the coins off the ground and stuffing them into their pockets. 'We're rich!' Morgan shouts.

'Bonehead!' Jack says, and he kicks me. As he does, one last coin drops from the leg of his pants to the ground, and I swoop on it before he does.

'Gimme that!' Jack demands, but I back away quickly, rubbing the moisture off the coin and holding it up in the sunshine. Our last two bucks. It glints like a magical nugget of hope . . . and it fills me with a possibly brilliant idea.

'Do you reckon, if I bought Sasha a sausage roll with sauce for her birthday, that'd be enough to make her want to go out with me again?'

Jack growls, runs at me and mashes me into the ground.

RARNALD THE RAT

Rarnald the Rat is my best non-human friend. (And sometimes I like him better than I like Jack.) Rarnald has been on the run in our house for years. No matter what Mum does, she cannot catch him. He is Indestructo-Rat, with a heart as big as a horse. Tonight, though, she has had it up to here with him (about halfway up her forehead). She says Rarnald is going down, and I'm on a desperate mission to save him.

When I was little, Rarnald and I were besties. We did everything together.

Exercise.

Make each other laugh.

Eat snacks.

Perform tricks.

Rarnald was awesome. *Is* awesome. He's about five years old now, which is pretty old in rat years. If he were human he would have a hearing aid and his pants pulled up under his armpits. But he looks after himself.

Me and Rarnald
(ah, good times...)

'Stop encouraging that rat, Tom!' Mum has always said. 'Rats are disgusting. They're a health hazard. Wash your hands.'

Rarnald heard he was a health hazard.

'But he's my friend.'

'Don't be silly. Boys cannot be friends with rats. Go and get some real friends.'

So she set a trap. Not a Buddhist rat-trap that catches the rat alive but a giant, vicious rat-smacker. That's how angry she was. She put a chunk of tasty cheese in it, which I thought was pretty funny.

'What are you laughing at?' she snapped as she pried back the metal smacker.

'Nothing,' I said.

Rarnald didn't eat tasty cheese. He only liked Jarlsberg. But Mum did not need to know that.

She checked the trap every morning for weeks. 'Still hasn't taken the bait. Maybe it's gone,' she said.

'Yeah. Maybe,' I said, breaking a chunk of Jarlsberg off the wedge in the fridge and heading to my room.

'no, I only eat Jarlsberg old chap.'

For a while, life was sweet. My friend was safe. I even built him a little hutch out of Lego.

But, tonight, Bryce is over for dinner and I'm praying that Rarnald lays low. Bryce Smith is a 'dental prosthetist', a false-teeth guy. Mum, for some reason, really likes him, but I keep kind of messing things up for them. Like the time Bryce gave me a job at the denture clinic and I stacked the delivery bike, spilling teeth all over the road, which were then run over by a garbage truck. Tonight, Mum has threatened me with death if I do anything wrong.

Dinner is going okay and Bryce has just begun a story about his recent trip to Hong Kong for a tooth conference.

'I was flying over Hong Kong Harbour, reading a fascinating article about bees,' he says, 'when, quite to my surprise . . .'

Mum is slicing up a lemon meringue pie for dessert at the kitchen bench and pretending to enjoy the story when she screams, drops the knife to the floor and leaps back.

Standing there on the bench, on his two hind feet, watching her, is Rarnald.

'Tom!' she snips.

'Yes,' I squeak.

'Come. And. Get. This. Raaaaaaargh!'

Rarnald makes a run for it. He scampers past the fruit bowl, executes a perfect swan dive off the kitchen bench, grabs the curtains in his tiny claws, swings to the ground, dashes under the dining table, making Bryce jump (and squeal, I might add).

Rarnald skids around the corner into the lounge room and slides, cool as anything, under the couch.

I breathe a sigh of relief.

Mum and Bryce stare, horrified.

I am so proud of Rarnald. He's a total action hero. I want to see it again in slo-mo.

'I'm sorry about that, Bryce,' Mum says, glaring at me. 'Would you like dessert?'

Ramald's going to be in THE rat Olympics one day.

Bryce swallows hard and politely says yes. He makes a joke about rat meringue pie, which I don't find funny at all. Mum and Bryce eat a few bites, but I can tell that the night has turned sour. Then Bryce puts down his spoon and says, 'Darling, would you like some help catching that rat?'

Okay, two things:

1. Bryce calling Mum 'darling' is weird and wrong.

2. After he just squealed, I hardly think he's

in a position to offer to catch a rat as intelligent and nimble as Rarnald.

Mum flicks a knife-like glance at me. She wants to say no to Bryce's offer. She wants to forget it ever happened. I want her to say no. But she doesn't. She says yes. Bryce stands from the table, claps his hands together and wiggles his bushy black-and-silver eyebrows.

'Now,' he says, heading into the lounge room as though he is about to Sumo wrestle my rat. 'Help me move the couch please, Tom.'

I look to Mum. Her eyes widen and she jerks her head towards the couch. She fetches the empty four-litre ice-cream container from beneath the sink.

I grab one end of the couch. Bryce grabs the other. I move slowly and make lots of noise, giving Rarnald ample time and warning to make his escape. But, when the couch is out, there he is, plain as day, surrounded by three-centimetre-thick dust pocked with marbles and twenty-cent pieces and my missing shin pad. Rarnald appears to be gnawing something off his bottom.

Mum closes in on her nemesis. Bryce moves in from the side. Slow and steady. I bump the coffee table and jingle the change in my pocket, but Rarnald continues to gnaw away on his backside like he's performing a lifesaving operation.

'This is it,' Mum whispers. 'Rarnald's last stand.'

'It has a *name*?' Bryce asks.

'Just focus,' she snaps.

Slowly, stealthily, she closes in, ice-cream container ready. Two metres. One metre.

Fifty centimetres. She is ten centimetres away from my friend, and I know that I have to do something.

I cough loudly.

Rarnald looks up, sniffs the air, then blazes a trail through the dust. Mum slams the container down, catching his tail. Rarnald squeals almost as loudly as Bryce. Mum lifts the container and Rarnald escapes – under the couch, across the floor, under the dining table, into the kitchen.

We give chase, and I just manage to see him commando-roll under the fridge.

'Move the fridge!' Bryce orders, marching past me.

'But –'

'Move. The. Fridge,' Mum says.

'Yes, Mum.'

I grab one side. Bryce grabs the other. Mum is poised with the container. This is terrible. Imagine if giant rats, twenty times our height, were hunting us down, sniffing us out, trying to trap *us* in enormous ice-cream containers. It isn't fair.

We wheel the fridge out. There he is again. Rarnald the Rat. Plain as day. Sitting in among the dust bunnies, roach baits and a couple of petrified vegetables. He is nibbling on a long-dead carrot, like he has all the time in the world. Has he lost his little rat-mind? I want to scream at him, tell him to wake up to himself, slap him across his furry snout. Why is he acting like this?

Mum moves in with the ice-cream container. Quiet. Careful. She holds it over Rarnald and, ever so slowly, lowers it. He has no idea, the poor little guy. I have to warn him.

I whack the side of the fridge and Rarnald finally drops the carrot. He looks up just as Mum brings the container down. He spins and slides, low to the ground, like a martial arts master. Rat-kwondo, maybe. As the container hits the floor, he runs right over Bryce's expensive Italian shoe. Bryce squeals again. Mum dives, faceplants on the kitchen tiles and misses him. I swallow a laugh as Rarnald scurries into the pantry.

'Bryce!' Mum hisses, peeling herself off the floor, wild and unhinged. 'Are you a man or a mouse?'

'A man?' he replies.

'Well, help me catch this rat! And if I hear you squeal again, you're out, okay?'

Bryce nods.

Mum flicks on the pantry light, ice-cream container ready. She scans the lower shelves, shuffles boxes and cans out of the way with her foot. I'm nervously hoping that Rarnald has an

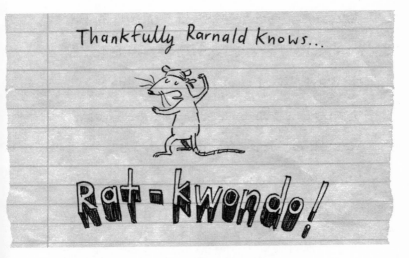

Thankfully Rarnald knows...

Rat-kwondo!

escape hatch at the back of the cupboard. Then, right down the bottom, I see a tail poking out of a hole in a giant pumpkin that has been there forever. Maybe Rarnald is hollowing it out for Halloween. The good news is that the pumpkin looks too big for Mum's ice-cream container.

She opens the fridge, grabs a piece of cheese. It is Jarlsberg, Rarnald's favourite. And it's a slice. I am going to be sick. Rarnald cannot resist Jarlsberg slices. He loves them even more than he loves chunks. Mum scooches down and leaves the cheese outside the hole in the pumpkin. She waits, container positioned right over the cheese. This is bad. Really bad. If he goes for the cheese he is gone. Gone-zo. Gorgonzola. And, if I know Rarnald, he will go for that cheese.

His tail disappears inside the pumpkin

and his tiny nose pokes out, twitching. The delicious smell is too much for him. Apart from diving in front of the container or grabbing the pumpkin and hurling it out the window, there is not much I can do. Rarnald's whole head is out of the pumpkin now. He is smelling that wonderful, wonderful cheese. He crawls down onto the floor. Beautiful grey fur, pink nose and ears. Can he not see my mother with her makeshift anti-rat contraption?

He crawls towards the cheese. This is it. Goodbye, my friend. Au revoir. Auf Wiedersehen. Ciao.

he smells cheese

MY friend RARNALD

Mum brings the container down, signalling the end of Rarnald's five years on the run, when, suddenly, nine tiny rats jump out of the pumpkin to join Rarnald at the cheese.

Mum breaks the Guinness World Record for Loudest Human Scream. She leaps a metre in the air, drops the container and flees to the lounge room. Bryce beats her there.

Rarnald has babies. Cute little wubbzy rat-babies. I watch them devour the cheese, then I stuff the entire family into my hoodie pockets and take the hallway exit down to my room. I squeeze the family of rats into Rarnald's Lego hutch and, as I do, I'm pretty sure he gives me a wink. Although I am now thinking that 'he' is probably a 'she', so I have started calling him, I mean her, Rarnalda.

The next morning I am grounded for 'aiding and abetting' a rat. I sell the baby rats at school for a dollar each. I explain to Rarnalda that I don't have space to keep nine mature rats safe and fed under my bed, and that they went to very good, rat-loving homes. I even ran background checks for snake owners. She understands.

Bryce does not return to the house for a while. My mother says that he is 'a big wuss'. I laugh when she says this, and she growls at me. Mothers are sometimes difficult to understand.

Rarnalda and I still exercise together. We still make each other laugh. We still perform tricks. Yep, Rarnalda the Rat is my best non-human friend.

What Would You Rather Do?

(Part 1)

When Jack stays over at my place, we stay up late playing 'What Would You Rather Do?'. It's a game where you are faced with two impossible choices, but you have to choose one.

What would you rather do . . . ?

* Kiss a dog or a cat?
* Have a finger chopped off or a toe?
* Get locked in a cage with a hungry boa constrictor or an angry gorilla?
* Eat a Ziploc bag full of your grandfather's toenails or eat a cereal bowl full of your cousin's scabs?

* Be eaten by a dinosaur or a dragon?
* Have chicken-pox for three months or nits for a year?
* Go over Niagara Falls in a barrel or fight Spain's toughest bull?
* Spend an entire year at school doing only your least favourite subject or spend a week in a jail for insane clowns?
* Eat dog poo or cat vomit?

* Get dropped into a pit of snakes or spiders?

* Drink a warm tuna milkshake or a tall glass of your own wee?

* Wear a T-shirt to school that says 'I love my mummy' or accidentally poo your pants at the beginning of a two-hour maths test that you are not allowed to leave?

OR

All of the above?

EVEREST

'I'm going to climb Mount Everest,' Nan says one afternoon at her kitchen table.

I look her in the eye. She does not look like she is joking. This worries me. My nan is a frail biscuit of a woman.

'Take a look at this,' she says, sliding a newspaper towards me and pointing to a small article at the bottom of page seventeen.

The headline reads: '73-year-old Japanese Woman the Oldest Female to Climb Everest.'

'I'm seventy-five,' Nan says, grinning, 'which means I can beat her.'

'But it's the world's tallest mountain. And you get tired baking a fruitcake,' I say. 'Look, it says here that this woman had climbed it before, that she broke her own record.'

'I'll train,' Nan says. 'You're never too old to learn something new, young man.'

44

I want to say, 'Well, sometimes maybe you are too old,' but I chicken out. Instead, I say, 'How will you get your walking frame up there?'

'Don't be a smart alec.'

'What?'

'I can see that look in your eye. You don't think I can do it, do you?'

I pause for less than a second, then say, 'Yes.' But she knows I'm lying.

'I thought as much. You think I'm old and crazy, but let me tell you something, buster: seventy-five is the new sixty-five. If that woman was seventy-three then my body will, technically, be eight years younger than hers, but I will still be the oldest woman to climb Mount Everest, according to my birth certificate.'

I think about this for a long time.

'I want you to help me train,' she adds. 'We start at five tomorrow morning.'

'Five? Why five?'

'Because, you ninny, that's when old people get up. I go to bed at six. You can't expect me to sleep more than eleven hours, can you? That's called being dead.'

'Um . . . I guess not. Can I have an iceblock?'

'Of course you can. Can you get your nan a Cornetto? That's a good boy.'

I slip out the back door, jump off the back veranda and head into the garage, to Nan's freezer full of iceblocks and meat.

I know I have to stop her. She'll kill herself.

I tell Mum about it that night while she is ruining dinner. My mum is good at lots of

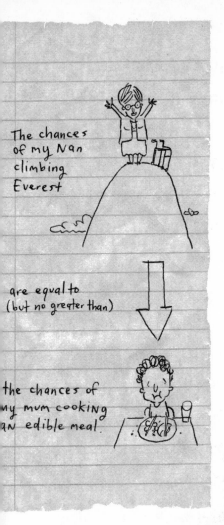

The chances of my Nan climbing Everest

are equal to (but no greater than)

the chances of my mum cooking an edible meal.

things. Cooking is not one of them. Every night is a lottery. It's exciting. And scary.

'She'll kill herself,' Mum says.

'I know. But she sounds really serious.'

'If I say anything she'll just dig her heels in. So you should just go along with the training and gently steer her away from the idea. Make her feel old. Offer to walk her across the street. Turn her hearing aid down.

Tell her I've been thinking about sticking her in a nursing home if she keeps doing crazy things.'

'That's not very nice,' I say.

'Neither is letting her freeze to death on the side of a mountain at eight thousand metres, or whatever it is.'

Click-clack-click-clack-click-clack.

It's dark and we're surrounded by thick fog as Nan charges full-speed (for her) up Cemetery Hill, pearl necklace rattling against her walking frame. This is the second-longest and steepest hill in Kings Bay. Ponka, her dog, runs along behind her, attached to a red lead. Ponka barks occasionally at shadows in the fog.

'Careful. You'll have another heart attack,'

I say, strolling casually beside her, but Nan keeps charging. *Click-clack-click-clack.*

'I've got three months,' she wheezes. 'If I don't push myself I'll never be ready to scale the south face in the Nepalese spring.'

In the distance there is a *hum-buzzing* noise that sounds familiar, but I can't remember where I know it from. The sun makes a feeble attempt to rise as Nan's wheezing grows louder.

'Nan, I really think you should take a rest.'

The *hum-buzzing* is loud now. I turn to see headlights through the fog.

'Car!' I call out, and Nan, Ponka and I move to the edge of the road. But the vehicle sounds too small to be a car. And it's going too slow. As it emerges from the fog I identify the noise. A motorised granny cart. With monster-truck wheels. It's hot pink. The numberplate reads 'SUE'. There's a screech of rubber on tar as the cart pulls up next to us. My best friend Jack's nan is sitting about two metres above the road in the hotted-up beast.

'Well, well, well,' she says. 'What are you doing out this early, Nancy? Shouldn't you be inside drinking a cup of tea with a blankie over your legs, listening to the wireless?'

Jack's nan is at least ten years younger than my nan – and twelve times larger. She is wearing jeans and a white T-shirt the size of a

save the whales

Jack's Nan is a very large Nan. The whale on her T-shirt is larger than a real whale.

parachute with 'Save the Whales' on the front. She has a tattoo of a lizard on her arm. Last time they met, Nan somehow managed to beat Sue in a back-alley brawl down near the nursing home.

'I'm training for Everest,' Nan announces.

Jack's nan laughs so hard she nearly topples off the cart. I take a couple of steps back. The fog slithers around and through my legs.

'You?' she scoffs. 'You must be a hundred and two years old. You'll be lucky to make it up this hill.'

'I'm seventy-five as it happens,' Nan says and starts walking again.

'Which is the new sixty-five,' I add.

'If you're going to climb Everest, I'll beat you there,' Sue says, driving along next to Nan.

'You're not as old as I am. You won't win the prize as the oldest woman.'

'I don't care. I only care about beating you. That's my prize.'

'You're on, you great heffalump,' Nan says.

'What?' I say. 'Nan, no! You're not climbing Mount Everest.'

'How about a little pre-Everest challenge?' Sue asks.

'When?'

'Two weeks.'

'Where?'

'Here. Cemetery Hill. First to the top and through the boneyard gates wins.'

I look at Nan, shaking my head. 'Let's just –'

'Two weeks today. Five am sharp. Bottom of the hill,' she says.

'You're on,' Sue agrees.

'Good.'

'Wonderful.'

'But you can't drive the cart in the race,' I stammer.

'Watch me!' Sue barks.

'It's fine, love,' Nan says. 'I'll beat her anyway.'

I shake my head. Jack's nan drives off.

'She'll smash us!' I groan.

'Maybe that's enough for today,' Nan wheezes. 'It's quite steep, isn't it?'

Nan is in the garage with her head in the freezer when I arrive at five the next morning.

'What are you doing?'

'Acclimatising,' she says, her voice muffled. She pulls her head out of the freezer. She has

NAN acclimatising for her Everest climb.

icicles hanging from her brows and her face is blue. 'It can drop to minus-sixty degrees Celsius at the summit.'

I take her inside, wrap her in a blanket and make her a cup of tea.

She guzzles it and says, 'Let's hit the gym. Bet I can beat you on the bench press.'

Nan lifts the barbell off the rack.

'Spot me,' she says.

'You sure that's not too heavy?'

She's lying on a weight bench made out of milk crates in the garage. She slowly lets the barbell down to her chest. I'm scared she is going to drop it and her guts will squish out of her ears. I try to help her lift it again.

'Let go!' she snaps. So I do.

She raises it, then brings it down again. This time she really strains to lift it. Her eyeballs swell and I worry she's going to drop it, but she doesn't. She presses it up to full arm's length, then down again. And up. And down. I smile.

'You're good,' I say. 'Let me get the camera.'

I run out of the garage, up the back steps and

grab Nan's camera off the dining table. I am only gone for ten seconds, but by the time I get back Nan is pinned beneath the barbell and her face is bright red.

'Nan!' I pull the barbell off her chest. 'Are you okay?'

I sit her up. She leans forward. I wonder if she has broken something.

'Did you get a picture?' she asks.

'No, Nan. I didn't get a picture.'

'Maybe tomorrow,' she says, standing up unsteadily, before flopping back down onto the milk crates. 'I might need my supplemental oxygen, love. Grab the canister and mask from under my bed. That's a good boy.'

The next two weeks are hardcore. Five o'clock, every morning. Weights, sprints on her walking frame, chin-ups. Meanwhile, across town, Jack is training his nan for Everest, too. They fit her cart out with snow tyres and chains. He thinks she's going to win. And she probably will.

One morning, on our way home from training, I try to talk Nan out of the whole Everest idea. 'I heard that it's best to attempt Mount Kilimanjaro first, that it's easier.'

'I don't have time for Mount Kiliwhatchamacallit. I'm seventy-five years old. I'll probably be dead before the year's out.'

'But Everest takes seven weeks. And, Nan, I read that with airfare, permits, climbing gear, sherpas and everything, it costs about forty-thousand dollars. How will you afford it?'

'I have a few dollars tucked away,' she says, tapping the side of her nose. When we get home she shows me all this money under her mattress. Some of the notes I don't even recognise. She reckons she's been sticking it there for thirty-five years. 'I never trusted banks,' she says. 'Or your grandfather.'

I tell her I've been reading on the internet about hypothermia, frostbite and how you can get sunburn in your nostrils from the reflection off the snow. So, next day, she

Nan's thermal underwear (made for the toughest indoor conditions!)

buys a whole bunch of stuff from the op-shop where she helps out on Tuesdays, including makeshift nostril protectors and thermal underwear (which she insists on showing me).

The night before the Battle of Cemetery Hill, this is the conversation at dinner:

'How's Nan?' Mum asks.

'Good,' I say.

'Is she still going to climb Mount Everest?'

'This is delicious,' I say, scooping up a

spoonful of cauliflower in ham sauce. 'Was this from a recipe or . . .'

'Tom?'

'Nah, she's given up,' I say.

'Why are you still going over to her place so early?'

'Just to . . . help her out. With jobs and stuff.'

Mum looks me in the eye. 'Are you sure?'

'Yeah. As if she's going to climb Mount Everest. She's not crazy!'

But Mum knows that this is not entirely true.

Oof. Oof. Oof.

That's what I hear as we make our way through the early-morning dark towards the starting line. Nan *click-clacks* along next to me.

It's a warm morning and I'm in thongs and shorts, but Nan is dressed head to toe in her op-shop outfit – sheepskin boots, ski goggles, knitted gloves, a ski jacket three sizes too big, a deer-hunting cap with woollen earflaps, and her pearl necklace and handbag. The part of her face not hidden by the goggles glows with sweat.

Oof. Oof.

We turn the final corner and, up ahead, in a pool of street lamplight, I see Jack sitting on the bonnet of his nan's motorised granny cart. He is holding a punching bag and Sue is smacking it with her bare knuckles like she's got something to prove.

When we reach the starting line I say, 'Racing in a motorised cart is cheating.'

Jack turns to Nan. 'Hey there, little old lady.'

Sue punches the bag one last time. Jack falls off the front of the cart and lands on his head.

'Ow.'

Sue's angry-looking black-and-white dog snarls at us from the back of the cart. It has a container hanging off its collar, like the small wooden keg you might see around a St Bernard's neck.

'All right,' Sue grunts, throwing a small Australian flag down to me. 'First one to plant their flag between the boneyard gates wins. And no foul play this time, you got it? On your marks . . .' She turns the key, revs the accelerator. 'Get set . . .'

'Go!' Nan calls, taking off into the dark, slightly faster than a snail.

'Get outta my way, numbskull!' Sue screams at Jack, who is still lying in front of the cart, rubbing his head. Sue jerks forward, rolling over his toe, squishing it beneath a monster-truck wheel.

'Owww!' Jack clutches his foot.

I run a few steps to keep up with Nan – she's really moving.

Beeep! Sue slams her hand on the horn. 'Outta my way!' she calls as her cart moves up next to us, headlamps lighting the road ahead. 'You haven't got a hope. And you look ridiculous in that outfit, by the way.'

Sue veers sharply to the left, trying to steer us off the road and into a ditch.

Nan adjusts her ski goggles but doesn't say a thing. She focuses on the road ahead.

'My dad was a world-class mountain climber!' Sue shouts over the annoying *hum-buzz* of the cart engine.

'What?' Nan lifts one earflap on her deer-hunting cap.

'I said my dad was –'

'I don't care if your dad was Sir Edmund Hillary,' Nan says. 'I can see you're a whopping great woolly mammoth riding a motorised buggy. How are you going to get that thing up Everest?'

Sue sneers. 'It's the Sherpa 5000, top of the

line. It's the Tenzing Norgay of granny carts.'
She floors the accelerator, taking the lead.
She veers in front of us and drops something off the back of her cart. I hear the tinkling of metal on tar and, in the red glow of her tail-lights, I see something sharp. Thumbtacks. Dozens of them all over the road.

I try to steer Nan around the tacks, but I'm too late. We walk right through them. Nan doesn't notice them in her thick-soled sheepskin boots, but my thongs are like a bed of nails.

'Ow. Ow. Ow. Ow.'

I want to stop and pick out the tacks, but Nan continues climbing so I suck up the pain and follow. 'Ow. Ow. Ow.'

'You okay, love?' Nan asks.

My thumbtacked soles go *click-click* on the road while Nan goes *click-clack*.

'Sort of,' I say, trying to ignore the pain roaring through my feet.

Sue is several metres ahead and mutters something over her shoulder to her evil dog. She reaches around and twists the lid of the container on its neck. The dog gives a husky snicker and leans forward. Something tips from the container and spills onto the road in a pool.

I'm distracted by Nan taking a huff on her asthma puffer.

'Are you okay?' I ask.

'Fine, love. You?'

She is sweating like crazy and starting to slow down.

'How about we take your jacket off, Nan?'

'No, I'm right. If I'm complaining about the weather now, imagine what I'll be like when I arrive in Nepal in May.'

'Aargh!' Nan screams and we both slip and fall on our backsides.

Jack limps past in the darkness, laughing.

My hands are covered in black stuff. Oil, maybe. Nan groans.

'Are you okay?'

'Just my hip, love. I'll be right. Can you help me up?'

I try to stand but I slip again before struggling to the edge of the oil slick.

'Grab my hand,' I say and pull Nan to her feet. She has black stains all over her new clothes.

'She's ruined my outfit.' Nan waves a fist at Sue. 'You beast!'

Sue scruffs her dog on the neck as the cart continues up the hill. She is about ten metres ahead of us with thirty metres to go.

'This means war,' Nan says, reaching into her handbag.

Sunlight colours the sky to the east and I can see the old iron gates at the top of the hill. Gargoyles look down at us from pillars on either side.

Nan hands me a small, paper-wrapped package. 'Plan B,' she says.

'But –'

'Do it!' she tells me.

So I do the thing we planned, even though I know it's wrong. I creep up behind the cart, careful not to be seen in Sue's rear-view mirror, but the dog barks like mad. I unwrap the package to reveal half a kilo of bacon strips, and saliva drips from the dog's angry, barking jaws.

I try to stuff one of the strips into the

chunky tyre tread as the wheels turn, but I almost burn the tips of my fingers off. I try again and manage to jam one strip of bacon in. Then two, three, four, five strips before the dog launches itself off the cart, barking midair, ready to finish me.

I stop, drop and roll away from the vehicle, down the hill. The dog hits the ground and I wait for it to maul me, to gobble me up like a strip of free-range bacon. But, instead, Nan's plan begins to work. The dog turns to the cart and bites one of the tyres in an attempt to get at the bacon. It howls in pain but then tries to bite the tyre again.

'What are you doing?' Sue screams at the possessed dog. It nips and

Jack's nan HAS an evil dog (but bacon is its weakness)

barks and bites until it is almost sucked up by the turning wheel. Then there is a hissing sound from the tyre, and the cart leans dangerously to the right.

Further down the hill, my nan wheezes: 'Take that!'

'That's not fair!' Jack yells.

Click-clack-click-clack-click-clack.

Nan catches up to Sue just as we hit the final steep section of hill. The last ten metres. Sweat storms down her forehead and sunken cheeks.

'Can't I take your jacket, Nan?'

'No, I'm fine,' she says, slurring her words. She shuffles forward, then falls. I reach out to catch her, but I miss and her head goes conk on the road.

'Nan!' I slip an arm beneath her and rest her head in my lap.

Nan needs oxygen when she does too much of anything. Like complaining.

'Thanks, love,' she says groggily. 'Feeling a bit woozy. You know, I didn't realise Everest would be this hard. We must be above 8000 metres. Have you got the oxygen?'

I unzip her enormous ski jacket and roll her out. 'It's okay, Nan. The race is over. We're throwing in the towel.'

'But Everest,' she says. 'I have to get to the top. I have to beat that vile woman. I have to be the oldest . . .'

'Forget Everest,' I say, looking up at the cemetery gates just ahead. 'It's over.' Looking down the hill, I see Sue's cart several metres behind us, not moving at all now.

'Help me down!' Sue snaps at Jack.

'But –'

'No buts.'

Jack pushes and shoves and squeezes his enormous grandmother off the cart. She staggers and falls awkwardly to the road. 'Help me up, you twit of a boy!'

'I'm trying!' he says. But Jack cannot budge her, no matter what he does. So Sue begins to crawl up the hill, groaning and scraping her way towards the top. Soon she is four metres behind us. Then three. Then two. She is like a maimed rhinoceros, inching her way along. I start to worry that she is going to roll right over us, mash us into the bitumen like road kill.

'Oh, no you don't,' Nan says, catching sight

of Sue. Nan pushes herself up and out of my arms, clutching the flag in her bleeding fist. I try to hold onto her but she slaps at my hand and starts to crawl up the steepest section of Cemetery Hill.

'I'm going for the summit,' she says. 'Radio back to base camp. Let 'em know.'

I laugh at her joke. Then I realise that it isn't a joke. I want to stop her, but I also don't want to take away her moment of glory.

Sue crawls past me, so close I can smell her sweaty armpits and coffee breath. She is right on Nan's tail. Nan doesn't have a hope.

Sue reaches out a hand, glistening with sweat, and grabs Nan's pearl necklace, pulling on it like reins to drag her back.

Nan makes a choking sound and Sue crawls forward.

My Nan has many speeds

stopped at
the lights

A leisurely
stroll

A brisk
walk

running like
the wind

'Go, Nan!' Jack shouts.

Sue heaves on the necklace once more and the pearls explode from around Nan's neck and bounce onto the road, rolling downhill. Nan will not be pleased. Those pearls were given to her by her own mother, Hepzibah Worboys, my great-grandmother.

Sue's hands land on a bunch of pearls, then the pearls roll beneath her knees and she scrambles and slips and squawks. Pretty soon, she's rolling back downhill on an avalanche of pearls.

'Help!' Sue screams, trying in vain to get a grip on the road. Jack and the dog look up and attempt to leap out of the way – but too late. They are pinned to the front of the cart by Sue's gargantuan body.

At that moment Nan claws her way

through the cemetery gates, plants her flag
and falls flat to the ground. Hunched gargoyles
look down at her as the first rays of golden
light touch her face.

'I've done it, Tom! I've done it,' she calls out
triumphantly.

'Yes, Nan.' I smile and bend down next to
her. 'You've done it.' I stroke her face, wiping
some of the blood from her forehead. I can't
believe it's over. My crazy grandmother thinks
she has climbed Mount Everest.

'Thanks for training me, Tommy.'

'That's okay, Nan.'

'Just think. In three months' time, I'll
be doing the real thing. I'll be on top of the
world!'

THE FIG

'Ewww, you've got poo on your back,' says a small voice behind me.

I turn to see a little punk with wingnut ears and a galaxy of freckles. He is staring at me.

'No, I don't,' I say.

'Yes, you do.'

'It's not poo. It's my birthmark.'

'What's a birthmark?' the kid asks.

Every year I dread it – the school swimming carnival. You're not allowed to wear a rash vest in races. That means my dirty, no-good, big brown birthmark in the middle of my back (which my best friend Jack calls The Fig) is on parade for the whole school to see. The kid with the wingnut ears looks like he's in Year Two. He's lining up behind me at the dive blocks, waiting for his final race.

'A birthmark,' I explain through clenched teeth, 'is a mark that you have from when you are born. Sorry if that's confusing for you.'

'Did the stork do a poo on you?' the kid asks.

The little girl next to him laughs. I do not. I want to pick him up and throw him into the deep end. Instead, I lean in real close.

'Did the stork do a poo on your face?' I ask.

The kid's smile drops. He looks at me. His bottom lip quivers. He looks like he's about to start bawling. I look around, worried that a teacher is going to see. Then he stabs a finger at me and shouts, 'Hey, everybody! Look at his back!'

Every kid and teacher within a thirty-metre radius, including the swimmers on the blocks about to dive in, looks at me – thirty or forty people, staring. Now my lip starts to quiver and I look like *I'm* going to start bawling. The starter gun fires for the race but only three kids dive in. The other five are trying to get a good view of my back.

I stomp on Wingnut's toe.

'Owwwwwww!'

I cover The Fig with my hand and make a beeline for the change rooms, marching all the way down the side of the Olympic pool. I can feel the crimson-red embarrassment of the kids watching and pointing and laughing. It's the longest walk of my life, and when I reach the change rooms I want to cry.

It is empty and the pale-blue concrete makes the place feel cold. I stand in front of one of the basins. I reveal The Fig and turn to look at it in the dirty, soap-smeared mirror.

'I hate you!' I whisper to it. 'You filthy, good-for-nothing swine. I'd probably be a swimming champion if it weren't for you. I wish you were gone forever.'

Unfortunate birthmarks in HISTORY

Mikhail Gorbachev   The Lone Ranger   Tom Weekly

I head into a toilet cubicle, slam the door, flip down the seat and slump onto it, head in my hands. In that moment I decide I will never go swimming again, never leave the house again, until I have had an operation to slice that thing off. In the distance I hear the starter gun go for the next race – my race.

'Hello, Old Thing,' says a faraway voice.

I bend down to look under the toilet cubicle door, but I can't see any feet.

'No, no, up here!'

I stand and turn to see a small animal perched on top of the toilet, right next to the flush button. It is chocolate-brown with a few black patches, two tired little eyes and a sad mouth. It looks like an oval-shaped cookie with tiny arms and legs.

'Rather nice to get a good look at your

face, finally,' it says. 'I had the impression that you might be ugly, but you're a handsome young man.'

I stare at the thing. If I didn't know any better, I would say it looks a little bit like The Fig. *A lot* like it.

'Anyway,' it goes on, 'I just wanted to say that there's no need to hate me. It must be difficult for you at times, having a large birthmark like me, but you and I are blood brothers. Together forever.' It gives me a wink. 'To hate me would be to hate yourself, and that would be just plain silly.'

'Who are you?' I ask. 'What are you?'

He looks at me like I am stupid. 'I think you know.'

I reach around and my fingertips touch the skin in the middle of my back. It is smooth.

No lumps, no bumps. It feels good.

'What do you want from me?' I ask.

'WHY is EVERYONE so unkind?'

my birthmark AKA The fig

'Nothing, Old Chap. I just want to reach out to you, to let you know that I feel your pain. I heard what that horrible child said to you out there and I, too, wanted to throw him in the deep end.'

You read my thoughts? I wonder.

'Of course,' it says in response. 'I think what you think. I feel what you feel. We are one and the same.'

Not anymore, I think to myself.

'I heard that,' he says.

I try not to think anything.

'Anyway, I just wanted to let you know that I'm watching your back, okay? Hug?' It stands on tippy-toes and holds out its little Fig arms, but I so don't want to hug it.

I run my fingers over the smooth skin of my back again and it feels so good. I know what I have to do.

I unlatch the door behind me.

'Where are you going?' The Fig asks, its sad little mouth turning down at the edges.

I hear footsteps and kids' voices coming, so I lock the door again.

'Please, don't leave me!' it cries. 'You weren't going to abandon me, were you? I was only trying to help. I've made a terrible mistake. I'll die. I need food.'

'Quiet,' I whisper. 'What do you eat, anyway?'

'Whatever you eat,' it says. 'And on that note, if you could steer clear of bread, that would be marvellous. I'm thinking of going gluten-free.'

'Who are you talking to in there?' a voice asks from the other side of the toilet door. It's Jack. There are lots of other voices in the change room now, too.

'No-one,' I say. 'Leave us alone.'

'Who's "us"?' Jack asks.

I look at The Fig, my lifelong shame. I could unlock that door and walk away now,

but I need to make sure it never finds me.
I won't sleep at night knowing that The Fig
is out there. And if it can read my thoughts,
it'll know where I am.

'Are you okay?' Jack asks. 'That was pretty
brutal out there, but no-one's talking about it
anymore. It's the last race. Just come out. Wear
a T-shirt.'

'Give me a minute,' I say, reaching around
to grab the toilet brush. I poke The Fig with it
and it dances out of the way. I stab again and
it hops to the side, hiding behind the half-flush
button. You might think a Fig would be frail
or sluggish, but this thing is agile and quick,
in peak physical condition. I swing the toilet
brush sideways, determined to whack him,
but he leaps over it easily, doing a forward
somersault and landing on his feet again.

'Help!' The Fig shouts.

'Help who? What are you doing in there?' Jack asks.

I look The Fig right in the eye. He is standing on top of the flush button. There is no way that thing is ever touching me again. I will finish him now. I move in with the brush raised like a lightsaber. I bring it down hard and fast, but The Fig dodges out of the way. I take another swipe but he ducks. Then I go *chop-chop-chop* with three fast little whacks, but he weaves. He pauses in a half-crouch, reading my next move before I even make it.

I try not to think. My gut takes over. I take one last swipe at The Fig and I make contact. It overbalances and falls into the toilet, just managing to hang on to the edge of the seat with one tiny hand. It's looking up at me, scared out of its mind.

'Help. Please!' it begs.

I rest one finger on the button.

'Please,' The Fig pleads. 'Don't flush.'

All I have to do is poke his tiny Fig-fingers with the brush, press that button and it will be gone. My shame will be no more. As I press down lightly on the button and the water begins to churn he looks into me, and I can't help feeling a connection. I can feel the panic inside him. It's like I'm looking into my own eyes, like I'm flushing myself.

His fingers start to slip from the toilet seat and, without thinking, I reach for his hand . . . but it's too late. He goes under the water and I panic.

His head emerges and he takes an almighty

Birthmarks as PETS...

Awww, he's soooo cute!

breath. 'Can't . . . swim, Old Chap!' he wheezes before the water swallows him again. This is horrific.

There are voices and footsteps outside, kids coming into the change room.

The Fig is down for a few more seconds before he resurfaces, thrusting a desperate hand up towards me. I reach into the grimy bowl, grab him, careful not to crush his cookie-thin body, and I haul him to safety.

There are lots of kids in the change room now, some in cubicles either side of me.

Jack knocks. 'Carnival's over. Let's go, man.'

I take deep breaths. I slowly open my dripping hand to look at The Fig, expecting to see his thankful little smile. But, instead, I find him crouched and angry. He growls and launches himself upwards. I try to catch him midair with my left hand, but he's too quick. *Slap*. He attaches himself to my face. I try to peel him off but he won't budge.

'What are you doing?' I ask, but he doesn't respond. 'I saved you!'

Nothing.

Another kid knocks on the door of my cubicle.

I scratch at my right cheek, trying to lift the edge of The Fig. I run my fingers over its rough surface. But it is stuck hard.

A head pokes over the wall from the next toilet cubicle. 'What's goin' on, Weekly? People need to go to the toilet.' I look up. It's Brent Bunder, the biggest kid in our year. 'Errr. What's on your face?'

I cover my cheek where my dirty-no-good-big-brown-birthmark is. I unlock the door and head out, slamming straight into Jack.

'What's up?' he asks.

'Hey, it's the kid with the poo on his back!' says Wingnut, the pipsqueak who started all this.

'It's *not* poo!' I scream. 'It's my birthmark. See!'

I rip my hand away from my cheek, showing

everybody. Forty boys fall silent and stare.
A couple in the back start to giggle.

'Is that funny? You wanna laugh at the kid
with The Fig on his face? You want a piece of
me? *Do ya?*'

Some of the boys look scared now.

'I was born with it and I'm *stuck* with it, all
right?'

Kids shift uncomfortably. A couple turn away.

'Sorry, Weekly,' Chris Meade says.

'I've never even noticed it before,' another
kid mutters. 'Has it always been on his face?'

I breathe hard, trying to settle myself as
the boys go back to getting changed. Jack
rests a hand on my shoulder. I touch my
face and turn to the mirror. It's worse than
I thought. I have to come to terms with the
fact that I might look like this forever. Or at

least until The Fig calms down and we can talk it over.

Wingnut shuffles forward and stands in front of me. He stares at my cheek.

'That thing is reeeally ugly. And how'd it get on your *face* anyway?' he asks.

I feel the anger rise up in me again. I want to throw him in the deep end. The Fig feels the anger, too. I know it. He's growing warm on my cheek.

'You want me to get a knife and chop it off?' Wingnut asks with a smile.

My cheek starts to burn and, in that instant, something magical happens . . .

The Fig tears himself off my skin in a fury and launches through the air towards Wingnut's face.

Part of me is ecstatic, but part of me misses my old friend already.

When I hear the satisfying smack of The Fig landing in the middle of Wingnut's forehead, there seems to be just one thing to do. I point and say, 'Ewww, you've got poo on your face.'

Wingnut's fingers fly to his forehead and he runs his fingers over The Fig's bumpy surface. He turns to the mirror, mouth open in horror.

'It's not poo!' he says, quietly crying. 'It's a birthmark!'

Just when you thought it was safe to go bACK in the water, in the dark, in an attic, at that abandoned place in the woods...

BIRTHMARK PICTURES
P R E S E N T S

THE FIG

HE'S EVERYWHERE! *

*Especially in foggy areas and places that are badly lit or smell kind of weird.

(also, don't open old boxes or play old VHS tapes - seriously!)

THE BABYSITTERS

'Ahoy, me hearties,' says a bored pirate voice over the speakers. 'No mates over the age of seven are allowed on the climbing equipment. Or I'll make ya walk the plank. Arrr.'

A Very Large Man wearing purple-and-black striped pirate pants pulled up to his armpits finishes the announcement and flicks off his headset microphone. He shouts at a kid who is wearing shoes on the giant inflatable shark.

'Dack!' a voice screeches from high above us.

My best friend Jack's three-year-old brother, Barney, is at the top of the highest slippery dip, waving to us like a madman. Jack rolls his eyes, forces a smile, waves back.

'That kid is so annoying,' Jack says.

Barney squeals down the yellow slide into a pit of colourful balls and disappears. I secretly hope he might not resurface. But he does, bursting from the balls and smashing his head on another kid's chin. The other kid starts bawling and pinches Barney on the neck.

'Happy birthday,' I say, clinking milkshake glasses with Jack.

He grunts.

Jack's mum had to work this morning so, even though it's Jack's birthday, she made us bring Barney to KidsWorld: a three-storey, pirate-themed indoor play centre. We have to

Barney.
A more
scurvy-dogged,
swashbuckling
maGGoT you'd
never meet!

keep him out till midday, and then we can go to the movies. That's the deal. So Jack and I are crammed into the Jolly Roger Cafe with about fifty coffee-guzzling parents tapping madly on their phones.

Up on the pirate ship dozens of crazy kids are firing cannons and climbing the tower that stretches all the way to the ceiling. Rain pounds the roof high above us. Happy pirate songs warble from giant speakers.

'I never want to have kids,' Jack says,

wiping milkshake from the corners of his mouth.

'Parents are so weird,' I say. 'Why do they do it to themselves?'

'Barney's bad now, but pretty soon he's going to be like us, and I definitely wouldn't want to be our parents with all the weird stuff we do.'

Barney pushes through the crowded cafe, red-faced, howling, snot cascading into his mouth.

'What's wrong this time?' Jack asks, slurping the last of his milkshake and looking at his watch. 'Actually, don't tell me. Ten to twelve. The movie starts in half an hour. We're going.'

Barney leans forward, opens his mouth and vomits on Jack. Bright-red creaming soda vomit. All down Jack's white T-shirt and jeans.

'No!' Barney screams. 'Not go home!'

Jack jumps up from the table.

'We have a vomiting incident at table sixteen,' says the Very Large Man over the speakers. 'Can I please have a pirate helper to swab the deck?'

Every single person in the cafe turns in our direction. I hand Jack a wad of serviettes from the middle of the table. He dabs at his neck and T-shirt.

'Why did you just vomit on me, Barney?' Jack says, barely containing his rage.

'BARNEY. NOT. GO. HOME!'

'I'm not asking about *home*. I'm asking about the vomit.'

'Barney says NO!' He shakes a balled fist at Jack like he is about to punch him.

A couple of mothers nearby try not to laugh.

Jack throws the serviettes onto the table and grabs Barney by the hand.

'No, you big Boobyman!' Barney shouts, stomping on Jack's foot.

Jack drags him out of the crowded cafe, squeezing through the maze of parents and prams.

'LET ME GO!' Barney shouts.

'Don't think so,' Jack says. So Barney bites him on the hand. Hard.

Jack screams. Barney bolts across the blue rubber mats. He throws himself at a rope ladder on the side of the pirate ship and scrambles up onto the deck, where he stops, wiggles his bottom at us, blows a big raspberry and races towards the climbing tower.

Jack chases him up the ladder onto the ship. I follow. A whistle blows and there is a voice over the speakers. 'Would you two scallywags please get OFF the ship!'

The VLM (Very Large Man) is pointing at us.

'Jack!' I say. 'We're not allowed.'

But Jack keeps going.

I look down at the VLM, shrug and follow Jack across the ship's deck to the bottom of the tower. It soars high above us – a three-storey colourful column of climbing tower with netting to fence the kids in.

'Jack, we're not allowed. We've got to go down. That pirate guy is scary.'

But Jack is already on his hands and knees, crawling into the bottom of the tower.

'Jack?'

He keeps going, so I follow him. The space is tight and twisty, made for kids a quarter of our size.

I'd like to send tHE VERY LARGE MAN to Davy Jones' locker!*

(* That's the bottom of the sea for all you non-pirate folk.)

'Barney!' Jack screams.

No response.

Just the wild cries of a hundred toddlers.

'He is so dead,' Jack says, knocking a couple of kids out of the way as he climbs up onto the first-storey platform. As I make it onto the platform I see Barney crawl into the bottom of a bright-red slippery dip tunnel that leads up to the next floor.

There is a shrill blast on the whistle. I look down and the VLM, with plastic sword drawn, is on the ship's deck below us, bounding towards the tower, his short sausage legs moving double-time. He points a finger at us. 'Arrr! You two scoundrels, off NOW. That be a one-way tunnel violation!'

'Jack, we'd better go down,' I say.

But Jack is already twisting his body into the slippery dip up to level two.

What am I supposed to do? Follow Jack or listen to the VLM, whose face looks ready to explode as he blows his whistle again. Parents in the Jolly Roger Cafe are watching us and pointing. I am not going to face them alone, so I follow Jack into the red slide. The tunnel is hot, moist and thick with kids.

I start to climb over them. I worry that I might get stuck. I panic and am about to back out when I see light ahead. I smell fresh air through the dense fog of toddler bum-stench. I see Jack's legs at the top of the slide. I press one foot to each side of the tunnel and climb, spider-like, over seven kids before throwing myself onto the next platform.

There is a blast on the whistle. I look down through the blue netting to see the VLM climbing an emergency ladder on the outside of the tower. I bet he's loving this. Guys like him wait their whole careers for something like this to happen.

I look around to find Jack. He's at the top of a fireman's pole. There are five or six fire poles in a variety of colours leading up to the third platform, the top of the tower. Most have

this place JOLLY well stinks !!

two or three kids on them, desperately trying to pull themselves up to the top.

I see a pole with only one kid on it. I peel her off, set her aside and start up the pole. Just then the background pirate music stops. The speakers squeal and kids below me clutch their ears.

'Would you two scurvy dogs please remove yourselves from the play equipment?' announces the VLM on his headset as he climbs the ladder. 'You may have the brains of five-year-olds, but you don't have the bodies.'

I heave myself onto the third-floor platform. It smells real bad up here, like farts and party pies. Twenty or thirty little kids shove each other and pull hair, fighting to get to one of the four slippery dips that slither down to the ball pit far below.

'He's coming!' I tell Jack.

All the kids look up at us like we're escaped criminals.

'What are you staring at?' Jack snaps at a three-year-old girl dressed in pink with a chocolate smudge for a mouth.

The girl starts crying.

'I'm dobbing!' another kid shouts, pointing at Jack.

'Belt up,' Jack says. 'I just want my brother.' He moves, slow and steady through the kids, towards Barney. 'We're going home, you little brat!'

'Barney says NO!'

'It's my birthday, and Tom and I need to be at the movies in twenty-three minutes.'

'You stupid pumpkin pizza head!' Barney screams.

'Leave him alone!' shouts a four-year-old boy with an eye patch and a scowl. He steps in front of Jack and raises his pirate hook hand.

'The jig is up,' says a voice. I turn to see the VLM unlock and unzip the emergency opening at the side of the platform.

'You're a naughty boy!' the kid with the hook says to me, pointing.

Then all the other rugrats join in, chanting, 'Naugh-ty! Naugh-ty! Naugh-ty!'

'Barney, let's go!' Jack demands.

'NO!' He looks wide-eyed and crazy, with creaming soda vomit all over his shirt.

'Barney!'

'No!

Jack moves to grab his brother.

That's when I hear a ripping sound. Velcro. A three-year-old girl to my left is holding a yellow-stained nappy. Steam rises from it.

'Wee-wee on your head,' she says, laughing.

'Wee-wee! Wee-wee!' a couple of others chant.

Jack takes Barney by the wrist and there is another ripping sound. A red-headed two-year-old is also holding a nappy. This one has poo in it.

'Whoa,' Jack says, letting go of Barney. 'No need to get weird.'

Rip, rip, rip, rip. Another four nappies. Two with poo, one with wee and one with something I can't even recognise. Some of the nappies look so heavy the kids can barely hold them up.

They move towards us, an army of angry, armed toddlers. Jack and I back off.

'Show's over,' says the VLM.

Three storeys below, a crowd of worried parents looks up at us.

One kid throws his nappy and it smacks Jack in the face. It is only wee, luckily.

'Hey!' Jack shouts, pointing at the kid. 'You're going down!'

Another kid throws her nappy. Poo this time. It drills Jack in the chest, right in the middle of the red vomit stain on his white T-shirt. It looks like modern art.

'Hey!' I shout. 'That is not cool.'

Right away I wish I hadn't spoken. The toddlers turn on me. A brick-heavy wee-nappy hits me in the guts. Then a poopy one splats me in the ear and slides down onto my shoulder.

The VLM watches on, a mean smile creasing his lips.

I'm hit in the back by another missile as I dive onto the slippery dip. Jack jumps onto the one beside me and we glide, side by side, down into the colourful ball pit below.

The last thing I hear is a kid screaming, 'Bye-bye, Poo-poo Heads,' before I disappear beneath the surface of the balls.

Everything is quiet. It is good down here. I hope they never find me. I want to stay down here forever.

BOOOM! An explosion and my face is pinned to the floor. My skull is being crushed, and I am pretty sure I will never breathe again. It is something big and soft, like a beanbag. But heavier. So much heavier.

It is the VLM's enormous backside. It finally rolls off and I suck in an almighty mouthful of air. A very large hand plucks me out of the balls and, for a moment, I remember the terror of being born.

Jack and I are suddenly face to face with the VLM.

'I've been looking for you,' he says in a husky voice.

He is so close to my face I can see the red blood vessels and giant blackheads on his nose.

'You filthy buccaneers deserve the cat-o'-nine-tails.' The VLM looks up to the top of the tower where the kids are laughing at us. He presses a button and speaks into his headset. 'Could I have a pirate helper to swab the poop deck, please? Pirate to the poop deck.'

The VLM drags us out of the ball pit and parades us past the parents. Some of them actually clap, congratulating him on his arrest.

'Wake up to yerselves,' a dad shouts.

'You frightened the life out of those kids,' says a mother.

'*Us*? Did you see them hurling nappy grenades?' Jack asks. 'We were under siege!'

The VLM leads us into a back room. We sit there, covered in goop, while he calls Jack's mum. Barney is brought in by a lady wearing an eye patch and a skull-and-crossbones bandanna.

'I'm thirsty,' Barney whines.

Jack is ready to explode.

'Can I have a creaming soda?' Barney asks.

'No!' Jack snarls.

'You can have whatever you like, darling,' the lady says, sneering at Jack, 'after that terrible ordeal.' She takes Barney off to the cafe to get his drink. Barney grins at us over his shoulder.

'Worst. Birthday. Ever,' Jack grunts.

His mum arrives a few minutes later. She is not as happy as she could be.

From the 'Wow, I didn't know that!' files...

Creaming soDA looks the same BEFORE

AND

AFTER it's been consumed. (crazy, right?)

I climb into the back seat with Barney. Jack gets in the front, and she says, 'I ask you to do one thing. One thing!'

'On my birthday!' Jack says.

'Well, I'm sorry the whole world didn't

stop for you. I had to do some work so that I can put a roof over your head and food on the table. Oh, and you can forget about going to the movies.'

'*What?*'

She reaches her hand through to the back seat and squeezes Barney's foot as she drives off. 'I'm so sorry I left you with these awful boys. I thought I could trust them. Do you want some of Jack's birthday cake when we get home?'

'Yes please, Mummy,' he says.

'This is so unfair!' Jack shouts, giving Barney an evil glare.

Barney pokes out his tongue, grins and says, 'Happy birthday, Dack!'

Jack's head explodes all over the front seat.

Don't
(A Day in the Life of Me, Tom Weekly)

'Don't wake up too early, Tom.'

'Don't be too noisy when you do wake up.'

'Don't use your bed as a trampoline, Tom.'

'Don't watch TV or play Lego before school.'

'Don't sneak into the chocolate cupboard
and eat Caramello Koalas before breakfast.'

'Don't eat seventeen Weet-Bix.'

'Don't dribble milk down your chin.'

'Don't burrow your hand to the bottom
of the cereal box to get the Shrek pencil
sharpener.'

'Don't read comics while you're eating breakfast.'

'Don't take forever on the toilet.'

'Don't read comics on the toilet.'

'Don't forget to shower.'

'Don't put the soap in your bottom.'

'Don't wee all over the glass in the shower to clean it.'

Not a good idea.

'Don't sing in the shower.'

'Don't moonwalk in the shower.'

'Don't do ballet in the shower.'

'Don't use your sister's expensive shampoo as a bubble bath.'

'Don't scrub your toenails with your sister's toothbrush.'

'Don't wipe your bottom with your sister's towel.'

'Don't forget to brush your teeth.'

'Don't just let the tap run for two minutes and pretend you've brushed your teeth.'

'Don't try to wiggle perfectly good teeth just to get cash from the tooth fairy.'

'Don't forget to make your lunch.'

'Don't pour hundreds of Mini-Wheats into your lunch box like they do on the ad. They're

expensive and the people in the
ads get them for free.'

'Don't put six slices of
cheese on your sandwich.'

'Don't make jam
sandwiches.'

'Don't make Vegemite
and lettuce sandwiches.'

'Don't make peanut butter-
honey-jam-Vegemite-banana-Nutella-bacon
sandwiches.'

'Don't make six sandwiches just so you'll
have mouldy ones to show Jack in two weeks'
time.'

'Don't forget to make your sister a
sandwich if you're making one for yourself.'

'Don't lick your sister's sandwich or rub it
under your armpit before you wrap it.'

'Don't let the dog lick your sister's sandwich.'

'Don't go to school if you have a virus.'

'Don't go to school if you have nits.'

'Don't go to school if you have a brain.'

'Don't go backchatting your teachers.'

'Don't go outside the school grounds at lunchtime.'

'Don't go into the girls' toilets again.'

'Don't scab canteen money off other kids.'

'Don't give horsey-bites.'

'Don't give horsey-bites to kids you've scabbed canteen money off.'

'Don't miss your bus home.'

'Don't watch TV all afternoon.'

'Don't make traps to injure your sister as she enters the house.'

'Don't fight with your sister.'

'Don't throw hamburgers at your sister.'

'Don't call your sister a stinky-poo-pants.'

'Don't laugh.'

'Don't move.'

'Don't breathe.'

'Night, Tom. Sleep tight.'

Kids Stink

'Seriously, you do not want to hear what my grandfather has to say.'

I was standing at the bus stop in front of my school. All the other kids were on the bus already.

'We are all different, Tom,' said my teacher, Miss Norrish. 'That's why we're participating in Living Libraries. To preserve the wonderful variety of voices in our community.'

'But, please, not my pop.'

'Yes, your pop, too. Each student has been

assigned a nursing home resident.'

'Well, can't someone else have him?' I asked. 'He's inappropriate. Mum reckons he's not even the same species as us.'

'Tom, of course your grandfather is the same species as us. Hop on the bus. We're late.'

I stared at her. Miss Norrish clearly did not understand.

She gave me a gentle shove.

So I did. I hopped on the bus.

This is a story from a while back, before Pop broke out of the nursing home, before he almost won the hot-dog eating contest. Before he died.

'Cliff Weekly.' That's what the sign on the door said. I stood at the end of a long white hall in the nursing home. It echoed with sounds of TV, a squeaky dinner trolley and the happy voices of nurses doing their rounds. The other kids from my class had already started interviewing the old folks.

I took a deep breath and opened the door. Pop was asleep in the chair by the window, mouth open, saliva stretching between his top and bottom lips.

He was only wearing undies. Bright yellow ones. Pop refused to wear anything but undies. They changed the nursing home rules for him after the Uprising, when the other inmates started getting around in their undies, too. But if he went out in the hall he had to wear pants. That was the new rule. So Pop never left his room anymore.

I hadn't seen Pop for a few weeks. Visitors were not his favourite thing. He always told them to . . . I probably shouldn't say. He always told them to go away, just not as politely.

'Pop?'

Nothing.

I stepped into the room. 'Pop?'

Still nothing.

Maybe he's dead, I thought. I wasn't proud of it but part of me was relieved. If he was dead he couldn't say the things

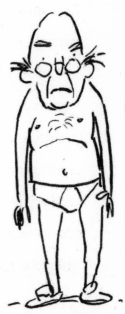

he would say if I interviewed him. Then my whole class and my teacher wouldn't have to hear any of it and I wouldn't be sent to the principal's office.

'Pop?' I said it quietly one more time just to be sure.

No response. *Oh, joy.*

This was terrible news. But such good timing. I would really miss days like Christmas when he threw ham at the nurse and told Mum her pavlova tasted like soap.

But at least I wouldn't have to interview him. I turned to leave. I would tell a nurse that he had passed on to a better place in the night.

I stopped in the doorway and listened. Something wasn't right.

Snoring.

Dead people don't snore.

I listened carefully.

'Hello!' said a loud, cheery voice behind me.

I nearly swallowed my tongue.

'You're part of the school project, aren't you?'

'Um . . .' I turned to see a nurse – red-faced, unnaturally happy, about the same age as Mum.

'I'm Debbie. Are you any relation to Cliff?'

'Well . . .' I said. I wanted to say 'no'.

Top 10 Things MY Pop is angry about (not in order)

1. Mum
2. That 'the Sullivans' isn't on the telly anymore
3. Grapes
4. Binoculars ('nothing interesting is that far away!')
5. Birds ('they're too happy!')
6. That ABBA broke up
7. Kids
8. People ('they think they're sooooo clever - with their beady little eyes and mushy brains').
9. The Sun ('What the heck does it do all day?!')
10. Fruit ('I don't like the way it looks at you and says "eat me, I'm really good for you."')

'I bet you're his grandson. I can see the family resemblance.'

Part of me died when she said that.

'I'll just wake him up.'

'No!' I said, a little too fast. 'Don't do that. Let him sleep . . . Please.'

'It's time for his medicine.' She wrote something on his chart.

'Maybe I can just interview someone else? I saw a nice-looking lady down the hall. The one with the missing leg and the party hat on. Pop needs his sleep.'

'No, it's fine. He's –'

'No, it's *not* fine!' I said, raising my voice.

She eyed me. There was an awkward pause.

Pop gave a loud snort and stirred. He smacked his chops, raised his head and looked around.

'Guess who's here?' Debbie the nurse said loudly, leaning close to Pop's good ear.

'Osama bin Laden?' Pop asked.

'No, your grandson.' She propped him up with a pillow and looked at the name tag on my jumper. 'Tom!'

'Great,' said Pop, but not in a good way. 'Has he brought that woman with him?'

'Mum?' I asked.

'She put me in this place and they're trying to kill me.'

'Take your medicine,' Debbie said sweetly.

'See! They put poison in it to try to make me less angry. But I've always been angry. There's no medicine for that. Anyway, what are you here for? Come to steal my money?'

'No, Pop, I –'

'Well, I lost it in The War. The commies

130

me → MY pop ←

took all of it,' he said. 'Apart from that, it was quite an enjoyable war.'

'I've got to interview you . . . for school.'

His face lightened. Pop loved being the centre of attention. Each year in the lead-up to Fast Eddie's Annual Hot Dog Eat he'd be interviewed by the local paper – and he kept every single clipping in a scrapbook.

'Why didn't you say so? Sit down!' he said with a smile.

I sat on his footrest. 'I have to record it,' I said. I dreaded pressing that button.

'Good.'

'I've got some questions.'

'Fire away.'

I hit 'Record'. 'What do you think is the greatest challenge facing our society?'

Pop thought for a moment then said, 'Kids. I hate kids.'

'You hate them?'

'Yep. Kids stink. They're disgusting. It used to make me physically ill when your mother had her nappy changed. I never did it myself, but even from the next room – the smell of it! You wouldn't believe.'

'So you think *kids* are the greatest challenge facing our society?'

'Yep,' he said, looking me in the eye. 'They have head lice, too. You probably have them now, don't you? You're probably infecting me with them.'

'I don't have nits,' I said, lying.

'That's another reason I hate kids – they lie all the time. Anything to get a lolly or an iceblock. Let me ask you a question: am I a nice person?'

I swallowed hard. 'Yes.'

'Liar!' he shouted, then laughed hysterically. 'Another thing I don't like about kids is how small they are. I mean, look at you. You're like a scary little garden gnome. And kids have so much energy, screaming and running around and laughing their heads off while the rest of us get on with the serious business of life.' He leaned forward in his chair. 'Imagine if adults carried on like a pack of galahs all the time. Nothing would ever get done.'

'What do you do every day, Pop?' I asked.

He chewed on the corner of his mouth.
'Well . . .' He licked his lips. 'Well, I just sit
here. They won't let me out. I've got a million
things I could be doing. Like getting ready
for next year's Hot Dog Eat, but they won't
feed me hot dogs in here. They say they have
sodium nitrites and sodium triphosphates in
them that will kill me. But if death is my ticket
out of here, I'll take it.'

'Pop, don't say that.'

'Here we go. Another do-gooder. That's
another problem with kids. Always trying to
be nice. Did I ever tell you that I try to run
them down when I'm out in my car?'

'Pop.'

'You know those school zones that tell you
to go forty? Well, I speed up and go eighty,
hoping to knock a few of the little ratbags over.'

'That's terrible, Pop.' I thought about pressing 'Stop' on the recorder.

'What's terrible is that I always miss them. Never the right time of day. What time does school let out?'

'Three twenty-five.'

'Right. Got it.'

'But you don't have a car, Pop.'

'Yes, I do.'

'No, you're in a nursing home now. Remember?'

A guide to the MANY moods of my pop

thrilled   overjoyed   pensive   serene

'Don't be an idiot, boy. I know where I am. Go and get me a beer out of the fridge. The cold ones are in the door.'

I looked around the room. 'You don't have a fridge.'

'Not in here. In the garage! Oh, forget it. I'll get it myself. Kids!' He tried to stand but stopped halfway up, his face pulsing red, eyes bulging. He clutched at his back.

Debbie the nurse dropped the bedsheets she was folding and came to the rescue. 'Just sit down, Cliff. Everything's going to be okay.'

'Don't mollycoddle me!' He slapped at her hand and lowered himself gently back down into the chair. 'I have a plan to break out of here,' he whispered loudly to me.

'I heard that, Cliff,' said Debbie, smiling.

'Good. I want you to help me.'

I decided to change the subject. 'What are some of the good things about our society?'

'Good?' he asked.

'Yes. Good. Like, what are you happy about?'

'You can find joy in every moment if you look for it,' Debbie said, shaking a pillow into a pillowcase.

'Bah! What have I got to be happy about? I'm surrounded by twits and incompetents. I always have been my whole life. Why don't people just see the world like I see it?'

I leaned in, wondering if Pop was about to share something personal.

'For instance, what's the point of whales?' Pop asked.

'The country?'

'No. Whales! The fish, you nincompoop.'

'I don't know.'

'Exactly. Stupid animals, they are. And yet you've got those imbeciles gettin' around in their rainbow T-shirts, throwing eggs at whaling boats. But what's the point of whales?'

'Well . . . they're an endangered species,' I offered.

'Ohhh, here we go. They've got you in their clutches, too, have they? Hippies. Let's all be happy. Save this, save that. The world's going to end. Well, I wish the world would end so I wouldn't have to listen to any more of this "Save the Whales" cra–'

'Pop, you're not really allowed to swear.' I stopped recording.

'In my day a person could swear all they liked.'

'But this is for school.'

'So?'

'Were you allowed to swear at school?' I asked.

'Of course. That was one of the subjects. Latin, Mathematics and Foul Language.'

'Yeah, right,' I said.

'It's true. They taught us some ripe words, too. I could tell you a couple if you like.'

'Cliff!' Debbie snipped.

pop's books
at school

'Not just poo-poo and wee-wee either. Let me see, there was . . .'

I clicked 'Record' again. This was getting interesting.

'Cliff, I forbid you to –' Debbie began.

Pop blurted a rude word.

'Cliff!'

And another one.

'How's everything going in here?' said a voice. I turned to see my teacher, Miss Norrish, standing in the doorway.

Then Pop said the worst word of all.

Miss Norrish's jaw dropped. She raised a hand to her mouth.

Silence.

'This is Tom's grandfather,' Debbie said, glaring at Pop.

'Is that another rotten nurse?' Pop asked,

squinting. 'What are you going to stick into me today?'

'I'm Tom's teacher,' Miss Norrish said, eyes wide.

'Oh, you look very pretty.' Pop brightened.

'Pop!'

'What? I'm not getting any younger.'

I covered my face with my hands.

'Well, thank you,' Miss Norrish said. 'Tom, time to go!'

I hit 'Stop'. 'Thanks, Pop. See you next week.'

'Don't bother coming,' he said, cranky again.

'But –'

'Not unless that teacher of yours is coming.'

'Bye, Pop.'

'Get lost.'

'So how did it go today?' Miss Norrish asked as we walked up the hall. The other kids from my class were waiting near the nursing home entrance.

'Well . . .'

'Your grandfather seems like an interesting man. Let's go back to school and have a listen.'

'Um, I think I forgot to press "Record".'

'Don't be silly. I'm sure it's a wonderful interview. You can be first cab off the rank when we get back.' Miss Norrish paused. 'He didn't use that language all the way through, did he?'

I searched for the 'Delete' function on my recorder. We walked past room after room of old people sitting in their chairs by the window, mouths open, saliva hanging between their jaws, snoring.

I realised that half of these people would never be heard again, except by the nurses. Most of them didn't even have flowers.

I looked at my recorder. I rewound and pressed 'Play'.

'No. Whales! The fish, you nincompoop,' said Pop's voice on the recording.

I hit 'Stop' and looked at Miss Norrish. 'I guess there is no-one else who sounds quite like my pop.'

She smiled.

I stopped searching for the 'Delete' button.

What Would You Rather Do?
(Part 2)

Jack slept over again last night. We stayed up till midnight playing 'What Would You Rather Do?'.

Here are a few of our best...

What would you rather do . . . ?

* Be sent on a mission to the moon or to the Mariana Trench, the deepest part of the ocean?

* Eat a TV or a door?

* Be stung on the tongue by a bee or have a llama spit in your mouth?

* Tell your worst enemy that you love them or your best friend that you hate them?
* Have a grand piano dropped on your head or be buried up to your neck in a nest of bull ants?
* Fly on a broomstick or a jet pack?
* Flush all of your money down the toilet or give it to your brother or sister?
* Eat a raw frog or sniff a farting skunk's bottom?

(continued)

* Have a whole jar of peanut butter massaged into your hair or a jar of Vegemite rubbed between your toes?

* Get shipwrecked on an island made of chocolate or marshmallow?

* Get shipwrecked on an island where the only food source is brussels sprouts or an island where the only food source is cauliflower?

* Live among the giants from Roald Dahl's The BFG or in a house with Aunt Spiker and Aunt Sponge from James and the Giant Peach?

* Have tongue sandwich for lunch tomorrow or snake head soup?
* Kiss twelve grandmothers at the local nursing home on the lips or skydive nude into the middle of a football ground at half-time on grand final day?
* Give a speech at school assembly naked or climb Mt Everest wearing only underpants?

MORRIS

BY RAPH ATKINS*

*My friend Raph, he's pretty awesome at drawing and making up stories. He asked me if I'd include one of his stories in my book, so I thought I'd cut the kid a break.

It is now official. I AM DOOMED. Very doomed. As doomed as doomed can get. And it's all the fault of my pet sausage dog, Morris.

All.

His.

Fault.

Morris THE sausage dog

I stood at the front of the class holding Morris for show-and-tell. His shiny collar glinted in the annoying, blinking fluorescent light. A silver triangle with his name engraved on it in fancy writing dangled from his collar.

All eyes were on me. Even the class pet Psycho, the evil goldfish that swims around in a bowl drinking his own wee, was watching me. I tried looking into his eyes to intimidate him. But it's hard to look into both of his eyes at the same time, because a goldfish has eyes on both sides of its head. So I ended up looking like a fruitcake, holding a fat, brown sausage dog, trying to intimidate a fish.

'Raph would like to show you Snot Bags, his rotten little dog,' Miss Brandy said to the class.

'Actually, his name is –'

'So you'd better listen!'

Miss Brandy is, unfortunately, our teacher. She is a rude, short, angry, annoying, lazy, green-haired woman of colossal size. At the end of my presentation I asked the class, 'Any questions?' A few hands darted up. 'Theo,' I said, pointing to my buck-toothed best friend, who was going to blow his sphincter if I didn't pick him soon. 'What's your question?'

'What does his poo look like?'

'Um . . .' I muttered.

'Does he smell other dogs' butts?' Theo asked. 'Does he roll in dead cane toads? Does he drink out of the toilet? Because I do!'

I looked away and decided to give someone else a chance. Before I could, Miss Brandy looked at her watch and snapped, 'Everyone outside! We're going to the hall for a special assembly.'

We walked out
obediently. Morris struggled
in my arms. I tried to hold
him still, but he slipped
free and ran across the
playground. I started to run

Psycho
The EVIL goldfish

after him. Miss Brandy grabbed me by the
collar and yanked me back into line.

'And where do you think you're going,
Raph?' she asked with an evil grin.

'To go ge–' I began.

'RHETORICAL QUESTION!' she
screeched, her face centimetres from mine,
spit projectiles pelting my face.

Morris continued running across the field
and disappeared into the Wetlands Nature
Reserve, a big muddy forest that grew next to

the school. We walked silently in two straight lines. But we weren't the only ones. Everyone in school seemed to be filing out of their classrooms and heading to the hall.

Roars of excitement came in waves from the kids inside. The teachers were running around, trying to shut them up, but it was no use. When we reached the hall I realised why.

Cameras clicked and flashed. News reporters scribbled notes. Others were having their make-up done. There were cameramen wearing big headphones, carrying massive, furry microphones, pushing each other to get the best position. Even the Prime Minister was there, smiling and patting kids on the head.

'What is this?' I asked Theo.

We sat on the cold, wooden floorboards,

waiting for something to happen. Our principal, Mr Bernard, walked onto the stage and stood next to a large bedsheet that was hanging from the ceiling. He held up his hand for silence. You could have heard a pin drop.

'Ladies and gentlemen,' he began, 'Prime Minister, esteemed guests, teachers –'

Then Theo farted. *BLAARB!*

'THEO!' screeched Miss Brandy. 'DETENTION!'

'Kids,' Mr Bernard said. 'We have some very special guests here today. They come from the local birdwatching team. I know you have all been busy studying about the Jagrofest in class, and how the last two of their kind are living in OUR Wetlands Nature Reserve. Well, now you – and the rest of the world – will witness, for the very first time, a live feed from the cameras that have just been installed in their nest.'

The birdwatchers stood at the side of the stage, grinning like madmen. Cameras pointed at them, clicking and whirring, as a massive round of applause rose from the audience.

'IT'S A WORLD PREMIERE!' Mr Bernard declared.

Grinning from ear to ear, our principal galloped down the steps and turned on the data projector balanced on a table in front of the stage. He typed into his laptop. Suddenly his desktop flashed onto the bedsheet, and the entire school started giggling. It had the usual icons running down the side – but his wallpaper wasn't what any of us had expected. I thought it would be something boring, like a times-tables chart. I was wrong. It was a picture of Mr Bernard and his wife at the beach, she in a red bikini and he in nothing but a hot-pink G-string. The colour drained from his face as his big, hairy bottom was beamed on live television around the globe. He muttered a few bad words and scrambled like a maniac to get his desktop off the screen. He clicked the mouse crazily, but that only made the computer freeze.

'AAAAAARGH!' he yelled. The image of the hot-pink G-string refused to come down. The Prime Minister tried not to laugh. Mr Bernard fumbled with the projector and wound up knocking it off the table. It fell towards the floor. He dived and caught it, crashing onto the floorboards himself. He rose to his feet, holding the projector in his

Mr Bernard
live on National
television!

quivering hands, and carefully placed it on
the table. He clicked an icon that looked
like a camera and the desktop disappeared.
Live images from the nest beamed onto the
bedsheet.

Everyone craned their necks to see two very
ordinary-looking brown-and-white striped birds
sitting in a nest of sticks and feathers, doing
nothing but peck each other in the backside.
The teachers went, 'oooh' and 'aaah'.

The chief birdwatcher walked onto the stage, hands behind his back, and stood next to the bedsheet.

'These birds are the last remaining male and female Jagrofests on earth,' he said matter-of-factly. 'I've been tracking Jagrofests for twenty years now. It's my life's work. I lived around these parts before I left on my lifelong journey, travelling the world in search of these wonderful creatures. Who would have known that I was going to be led all the way back to my home town?'

He looked as if he was about to cry.

And then he did.

He blabbered like a baby.

'FOLLOW YOUR DREAMS, KIDS! WAAAAAAAH! I DID AND I REACHED THEM! NOTHING CAN STOP YOU!'

A lady from the birdwatching team walked him calmly down from the stage. He was a sobbing mess.

The little brown birds on the bedsheet let out a good squawk and everyone sighed, 'awwww'. Then the nest started to shake. The birds squawked louder. Branches were cracking and leaves ruffled wildly.

And then it happened.

The end of my life as I knew it.

A brown, sausage-shaped dog jumped onto the nest and started snapping at the last two Jagrofests on the planet. The birdwatching chief screamed, got down on his knees and pounded the floor with his fists.

'MY LIFE'S WORK! NOOOOOO!' he wailed.

The audience gasped and my entire school

The last known Jagrofests
on EARTH. And Morris,
the sausage doG.

turned to me. Four hundred kids. Eight

hundred eyes. Glaring.

'What?' I said. 'That could be anyone's

sausage dog...'

The dog barked at the camera, a feather

dangling from its mouth. A silver triangular

name tag hung from its neck. Engraved on its

surface in fancy writing was 'Morris'.

'I stand corrected,' I said.

Morris bolted at the camera lens.

The chief birdwatcher bolted for me.

I bolted towards the door.

If you want to see one of your stories in my next book, send it to TheTomWeekly@gmail.com, and maybe I'll include it!

10 Funny Books

I love funny books, but it's super-hard to find a book that makes you laugh out loud.

Here's my top ten, featuring bums, billionaires and the world's most annoying baby brother.

1. *Funniest Stories*, Paul Jennings

2. *The Bugalugs Bum Thief*, Tim Winton

3. *James and the Giant Peach*, Roald Dahl

4. *Nicholas*, René Goscinny

5. *Eric Vale Epic Fail*, Michael Gerard Bauer

6. *SuperFudge*, Judy Blume

7. *Con-nerd*, Oliver Phommavanh

8. *The Really, Really High Diving Tower*, David Metzenthen

9. *Billionaire Boy*, David Walliams

10. The 'Just . . .' series, Andy Griffiths

TOM'S FUNLAND

'This'll be awesemic,' Jack says.

He is standing on the road outside my house searching for customers. I'm kneeling on the front lawn, writing the words 'Tom's FunLand' on a big piece of cardboard.

'*Tom's* FunLand?' Jack spits.

'I thought of it.'

'No, you didn't. We both did. It should be Jack and Tom's FunLand.'

'Jack and Tom's FunLand?' I ask.

'Yeah.'

'But that sounds dumb.'

'Only because it's got the word "Tom" in it.'

I add Jack's stupid name to the sign. It messes up the whole look of it. Now we probably won't get any customers and it will be all his fault.

'How much should we charge for admission?' I ask.

'Ten bucks.'

'Ten bucks?'

'Do you think that's too cheap?' Jack asks.

I look down the side of my house to the backyard theme park we have built this morning. In among the rides there are broken bikes, a rusty totem tennis pole, a dog-mauled soccer ball and an above-ground swimming pool that has not been used in five years.

'Fair enough,' I say.

I write '$10' on the sign. As I sticky-tape it to a tree I notice Mr Skroop, the world's scariest relief teacher, pruning his hedge next door. Mr Fatterkins, his enormous orange cat, sits on his shoulder. Skroop hasn't been getting much teaching work at school lately, not since he threw the whiteboard marker at Sam Stubbs and knocked out Sam's left-front tooth. But, then, a month ago, Skroop moved

Mr Skroop – the world's
scariest relief teacher.
(And his stupid cat, Mr Fatterkins)

in next door, which proves my theory that I am cursed.

'Hey, remember when he chopped your football up and posted it into your letterbox?' Jack whispers.

'Yeah. I remember.'

'And when he ate my scab.'

'Yes, Jack. I remember that, too. I watched him do it.'

Mr Skroop catches me staring. 'What are you up to, Weekly?' he rasps in a voice like twisted metal.

'Nothing,' I say, blocking his view of the sign.

He slithers towards me, trying to read the sign over my shoulder. He clutches the pruning shears. He has blood from a cut running down the fluorescent-white skin of his arm. Mr Fatterkins licks his ear.

'FunLand,' he says. 'Another harebrained scheme with that idiot friend of yours? Well, Mr Fatterkins is about to have his morning nap, and if I hear anything – *anything* – from this "FunLand", I'll call the cops. And then it won't be so "fun", will it?'

Skroop's favourite pastime is calling the cops. Last week he called the cops on the postman for not delivering his mail, but it turned out that no-one had sent him anything. Mr Fatterkins hisses at me and claws at the shredded wool of his master's maroon jumper. Skroop waves a gnarled dinosaur finger. 'The cops, you hear me?'

'Yes, Mr Skroop.'

He flashes his brown, gappy teeth and heads off, stopping at his front gate to glare at me. I'm pretty sure I see a forked tongue slip out of his mouth and back in before he slides up his white-painted front path.

'Nice guy,' Jack says. 'Wonder if he'd be interested in some work on our Haunted House attraction.'

'Two hours till Mum gets home. We better get some customers.'

We stand together on the kerb, searching, waiting. It's not long before Nick Crabtree and his little sister, Elsie, come by.

'You guys want to do something super-fun?' Jack asks.

'What?' Nick is a tall kid who always seems to have a large Slurpee in his hand.

Jack points to the sign.

Nick reads: 'Tom and Sack's FunLand.'

'Not "Sack". Jack!' Jack says.

I laugh. Jack punches me in the arm and

tries to scratch the curvy bit off the top of
the J.

'What's a FunLand?' Nick asks.

'Like a theme park,' I say. 'It's in my
backyard.'

Tom and Jack's FunLand

Clothes Line Carousel

Dog Rodeo

Burping Competition

Mayo Sponge Throw

Trampoline of Death

Jelly Slip 'n' Slide

Tree House High Dive

THE TRAMPOLINE
OF DEATH

Nick and Elsie look down the side of the
house to the yard. Nick takes a long sip on his
Slurpee. Elsie picks her nose and eats it.

'Come have a look,' Jack says. 'It's epic.'

Jack takes them up to the side gate to read the list of attractions sticky-taped to the fence.

'Cool,' Nick says. 'Where do we start?'

'You start,' Jack says, 'by paying your ten bucks.'

'Ten bucks?' Nick laughs and a small amount of blue Slurpee shoots out of his right nostril.

'Not per ride,' Jack says. 'It's an All-Day FunPass.' He smiles, which makes him look like a second-hand car salesman.

'I'm not paying ten bucks to play on a bunch of broken junk in Tom's backyard.'

'Okay, five,' Jack says quickly.

'No way.' Nick grabs Elsie by the shoulder to leave.

'Okay, two,' Jack begs. 'Please?'

Nick fishes around in his pocket and opens

his hand. He has a fifty-cent piece with a hunk of green chewing gum stuck to it, coated in sand.

'You can keep the gum,' he says, taking a long slurp on his drink.

Jack snatches the fifty cents and gnaws the gum off. 'You operate the rides,' he snaps at me. 'I'll go and find some proper paying customers.'

I swing open the gate and lead them into the theme park.

'A world of wonder awaits!' I announce, sounding a bit too much like Jack.

Elsie tries the Clothes Line Carousel first. Nick lifts her up and places her inside the springy seat that I've fashioned out of two

There's no such thing as 'old gum'.

of Mum's bras. I spin the rusty clothes line around as fast as I can. She squeals with joy, and I ask her to keep it down so she doesn't wake Mr Fatterkins. One of the bra straps snaps, but I manage to rig it up again.

Five minutes later, Jack is back with Mac and Lottie Rowland, two kids from down the street. Nick is on the Jelly Slip 'n' Slide. Elsie and Lottie hit the Trampoline of Death with the massive rip in the centre and a pot plant cactus underneath. Mac has a ride on the dog. They're all starting to have fun, and it's not long before Jack returns with four girls I have never seen before. They try the Mayo Sponge Throw. One pokes her head through the pool fence while the others chuck a mayonnaise-dipped sponge at her face.

'Is there any food for sale?' one of the girls asks.

'Um . . . yes,' I say. I race up the back steps. As I open the door I turn and look out across the yard to see our theme park in full swing. I can't believe that one of our crazy ideas is actually working.

In the fridge I find the meatloaf we're having for dinner tonight, an old onion, some taco sauce, half a brown lettuce and a withered turnip. In the pantry I find a box of cereal and a rusty can of creamed corn. Then . . . bingo! Half a packet of broken Scotch Finger biscuits and a Ziploc bag with seven lolly snakes from two Halloweens ago.

I fill some plastic cups with orange cordial, put them on a tray and head out onto the veranda.

'The restaurant is open for business!'
I announce and kids flock. Nick Crabtree buys all the drinks. Jack helps himself to the largest chunk of Scotch Finger biscuit. I whack him and the biscuit falls to the floor, but he eats it anyway. He tells everyone that the biscuits are a dollar each, fifty cents for one finger, twenty-five for a handful of crumbs. We end up getting ten cents a biscuit, which is close enough.

The two-year-old snakes are the bestseller. Twenty cents each. Jack auctions the last snake to the highest bidder and gets a dollar for it, then everyone hits the rides again.

'Weekly!' says a voice.

The smile fades from my face when I see Skroop and Fatterkins staring over the fence near the Sponge Throw. Skroop must be standing on a ladder. Either that or anger makes him levitate. He has a phone pressed to his ear.

'You have ruined Mr Fatterkins' nap time,' he shouts. 'He'll be tired for days. I am currently telephoning the police.'

'Watch out!' a girl yells, but it's too late. A sponge, thick with mayonnaise, cops Mr Skroop in the side of the face and spatters Fatterkins' fur.

Skroop lets out a strangled roar and wipes madly at his cat, turning the cat's fur into dreadlocks.

'Sorry!' I call out.

'Hello,' he barks into the phone. 'I'd like to report a neighbourhood disturbance. A riot at number forty-two Kingsley Street. I've just been assaulted with a missile . . . My name is Skroop. Walton Skroop.'

The side gate *screaks* and a gang of nine or ten kids from the neighbourhood wanders into my yard.

'Sorry, but we can't take any more customers!' I say.

'Relax. It'll be fine. I have an idea,' Jack says. He hits the kids for cash.

Secretly, this is the sort of missile I wish would hit Mr Skroop.

Suddenly, we have about twenty riders but only seven official rides. Queues start to form and kids complain about the heat. Mum's bra strap breaks again but I can't fix it.

The Slip 'n' Slide gets ripped and we run out of jelly.

'This theme park sucks,' Mac says. 'I want my money back.'

'We'd better pack up,' I tell Jack, who is running around with a lit match, lighting tiki torches underneath the Tree House High Dive. The torches are on bamboo poles taller than me, with thick white wicks poking from their tops. 'The place is falling apart. Mum's home in twenty-five minutes and Skroop just called the cops!'

'It's okay. Leave it to Jacky-boy,' he says. He lights the final torch, climbs the tree house ladder and makes an announcement to our disgruntled theme park guests: 'Attention please, Valuable Visitors! Welcome to our premier attraction, the one you've all been waiting for, the most dangerous and death-defying ride at Jack and Tom's FunLand – The Treeee House High Dive!'

Everybody stops and looks up at him. They do not look impressed. He climbs onto the handrail that runs around the edge of the wooden tree house platform, four metres above ground level.

'Watch me demonstrate a daring leap into the toxic, sludge-filled abyss known as Tom's Swimming Pool!'

He positions his toes right on the edge of the handrail. Twenty-five kids look on. A couple cheer. Others mutter about how shallow the sludge in the pool looks.

Jack closes his eyes, readies himself for the dive, flaming tiki torches all around. He lets go of the branch he is holding and leaps out

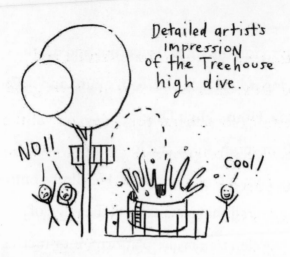

Detailed artist's impression of the Treehouse high dive.

NO!!

Cool!

over the pool fence. As he falls through the air, his foot kicks over one of the tiki torches. He executes a perfect belly flop into the bright-green cesspit, disappearing beneath the surface.

Kids gasp and gather around the pool fence.

'That bloke's a nutter.'

'Maybe he split his guts open.'

'What if he's dead?'

The naked flame from the tiki torch sets alight the crispy leaves of a dead vine hanging off the fence between Skroop's place and mine. Panic rises in my chest. It's never good advertising for a theme park when one of the owners dies on opening day, but I should also go and put out the fire.

Jack is still under, so I rip open the pool gate, climb the broken ladder, take off my T-shirt and scan the filthy swamp for any sign of life – only mosquitoes, thousands of them. I stand on the edge of the pool. I'm going to have to do this. I can smell smoke, but I figure Jack's slightly more important than the fence. I am poised to dive in when Jack bursts from the goop with a wild animal roar. He is the Creature from the Green Lagoon.

Kids cheer and queue up at the tree house ladder. Meanwhile, the small fire is quickly turning into a blaze.

'Fire!' I scream as Jonah Flem launches himself into the pool. I am smacked in the face by a thick gob of slime. Two more kids follow Jonah, flying out of the tree and into the pool.

'Jack, put it out!' I shout.

Jack, waist-deep in muck, turns, sees the fire and tosses handfuls of green slime towards it, but he finds it hard to reach the flames. I throw him a broken plastic bucket and he scoops sludge from the pool's surface and hurls it at the fire. But then the weirdest thing happens: the flames explode. The green gunk is feeding the fire rather than fighting it. The flames surge higher than the fence and they start to spread along the fence line towards Skroop's house.

Jack throws another bucketful just as Skroop's head appears over the fence. He cops the entire bucket of goo in the face. Green stuff hangs from his brows and flames shoot up at him. Mr Fatterkins screams and leaps off his shoulder.

'Fire!' Skroop shouts.

I run for the hose, twist on the tap and bolt towards Skroop. 'Outta my way!'

He ducks and I give the flames the full force of the hose. The fire cringes. Kids in the pool scream 'Over here!' and 'What about this bit?' and 'Let's get out of here'. I fight the fire for a full five minutes before bringing the blaze under control. By the time the last flame has been licked there is a large section of fence destroyed, creating a black, smouldering passage between Skroop's place and mine.

Kids look on. Jonah and Jack climb out of the pool. Others start to leave.

I turn off the tap and peer through the charred remains of the fence to check if Mr Skroop is okay. He walks towards me. He has ectoplasmic pool goop hanging from his eyebrows and mayonnaise in his ear. His clothes are soaking wet. His black hair dangles limply down his forehead.

'*You,*' he gasps.

I back up a little.

'*You* insignificant, flat-footed, jelly-back-boned, knock-kneed little prawn!'

'Huh?'

'Tom Weekly?' says a voice.

I turn to the side gate to see a police officer walking slowly through my yard, surveying the destruction: torn Slip 'n' Slide, smoking remnants of side fence, a bunch of swamp-creature kids escaping the yard as quickly as they can.

Pretty soon it's just me, the police officer and –

'Is Mr Skroop here?' the cop asks. 'He's made another complaint.'

Skroop steps through the gap in the fence. Mr Fatterkins is back on his shoulder, partly drowned, slightly charred.

'I am Walton Skroop,' he says, grabbing me by the scruff of the neck.

'I know who you are,' the cop says. He is a mountain of a man with a tree-trunk neck, who may have been a Viking in a previous life. 'You taught me in third grade. John Hategarden. You threw a piece of chalk at me, cracked the lens on my glasses.'

'Oh, yes,' Skroop says. 'Well, I'd love to chat but I have a crime to report. Thomas Weekly has been running an illegal business in a residential neighbourhood. He and his horrible little friends have assaulted me with mayonnaise, pool scum and water. They have set fire to my property *and* ruined Mr Fatterkins' nap time!'

Hategarden glares at Skroop. 'Do you have anything to add to Mr Skroop's description of events, Mr Weekly?'

I look around at what used to be my backyard. I'm usually a genius in these situations, but I can't think of any way to deny Skroop's claims. He has me right where he wants me. This grinds my teeth, churns my blood and gives my liver a Chinese burn. The best defence is good offence.

'It's his fault!' I stab a finger at Dark Lord Skroop.

Skroop tightens his hold on the neck of my shirt.

'And how is that?' Hategarden asks.

I look down. I have to come up with something. 'He's trespassing!' I say, pointing to Skroop's tartan slippers, standing in our backyard.

'You'll have to do better than that,' says the sergeant.

'He swore at me!' I say.

'I did not!'

'He called me an insignificant, flat-footed, jelly-back-boned, knock-kneed little prawn.'

'Right,' says Hategarden, making a note. 'Knock-kneed, did you say?'

'Yep.'

'What about the football?' I turn to see Jack crawling out from under the house.

'Oh, yeah,' I say. 'A couple of weeks ago, Mr Skroop chopped up my football and posted it into the letterbox.'

Hategarden stops writing and looks Skroop in the eye. 'Is that true?'

'The little scumbags should keep their sporting equipment in their own yard.' He scowls.

'And the scab,' Jack whispers.

'Oh, yeah. And, once, he ate my scab.'

Hategarden tilts his head to the side, as though he mustn't have heard correctly.

'*My* scab,' Jack says.

'Yeah, Jack's scab, but it was in my pocket. I was going to add it to my collection.'

'Is this true?' asks the sergeant. 'Did you honestly eat a child's scab?'

'Well, I –'

'Mr Skroop, you can't blame a bunch of kids for setting up a business in their own backyard. I remember you being miserable, but to call a kid a knock-kneed prawn, to chop up his football and –' Hategarden gags, as though he might be sick '– to eat a boy's *scab*, well, that is unforgiveable, un-Australian and possibly illegal.'

'In my defence,' Skroop wheezes, 'the scab was quite small.'

Hategarden grabs him by the arm. 'I think you'd better come down to the station and answer a few questions.'

'He destroyed my personal property,' Skroop whines. 'You'll pay for this, Weekly!'

'Save the Scooby-Doo routine for your statement,' the sergeant tells him and, with that, he leads Skroop out the side gate and down the driveway to the police car waiting in the street. He opens the back door and Skroop climbs in.

'No cats in the vehicle!' says Hategarden.

Skroop kisses Fatterkins on the nose and releases him on my front lawn.

A moment later the police car moves off up the street.

'Wow,' Jack says. 'That was cool.' He pulls a handful of change out of his pocket, counts out eleven dollars and fifteen cents for me and eleven dollars twenty for himself.

'Why do you get the extra five cents?' I ask.

'I came up with the idea.'

'No, you didn't.'

'Yes, I did.'

'No, you didn't.'

'Yes, I did.'

Jack heads out the gate and peels the FunLand list of attractions off the fence. He looks back at me, at what was once my backyard, just as Mum's car pulls into the driveway.

'You wanna do it again next Saturday?' Jack asks.

'Are you kidding?' I ask, closing the gate. 'Definitely.'

'Tom?' Mum snarls, popping her car door.

'If I'm alive,' I add.

Jack vanishes.

So our arcade didn't turn out quite as well as we hoped but don't let that put you off. It's an awesome idea and hopefully you learned a few lessons from our mistakes.

My Mistakes

1. Don't go into business with Jack.

2. Don't even become friends with someone like Jack unless you want your life to be a disaster.

3. Don't offer your sister's toys as prizes because she will bash you.

   (Unless she's a younger sister, then that's okay.)

If you were going to create your own backyard theme park, what rides would you offer? How much would you charge? What would the food be like?

(I recommend Scotch Fingers and Snakes, but buy heaps of packets.)

Email your backyard theme park ideas and drawings and I'll blog them.

I'm at: TheTomWeekly@gmail.com

I Think I Hate My Dog

I think I hate my dog.

I know it's a bad thing to say. I don't mean to hate Bando. He's a Labrador, so he's nice and everything. In fact, he's maybe the best dog in the world, ever.

But I still hate him.

Look at him over there, lying on his back in the middle of my bedroom floor in a puddle of early morning sun, paws in the air, half-asleep, waiting for his breakfast to be served. He doesn't have a care in the world.

Me? I've got to get up, go to school, hang out with my annoying friend Jack, do chores around the house, eat Mum's cooking, do homework, go to bed at eight-thirty. My life stinks.

And you know what the most annoying thing is? I get blamed for everything that goes wrong around here. The other day Mum's laptop screen was smashed, and you know who she pointed the finger at? Me.

I mean, sure, I did it, but I didn't even get a fair trial. I tried to tell Mum it was Bando, but she didn't believe me for a second. No-one would believe that the perfect dog could do anything wrong. I've had a gutful of it.

That's why I've devised my Ingenious Plan. I'm going to frame Bando for a crime. He'll get caught in the act and then he can start

It's about time Bando
did some Jail time.
(for crimes he didn't commit.)

taking the blame for some of the weird stuff
that goes wrong around here.

'C'mon boy!' I whisper.

I push myself up out of bed, tiptoe into
the hall, past Mum's bedroom door and into
the lounge room. The curtains are closed. In
the dim light I can see a ceramic bowl sitting
on a waist-high, white chest of drawers next
to the couch.

Man, that bowl is ugly. Poo-brown on the outside, yellow and green on the inside. Mum's favourite. I think she might have bought it from a garage sale, but she acts like it's a priceless antique. I agree that it's priceless, but only because nobody would pay anything for it.

'Stay,' I whisper to Bando. I creep through the lounge room and across the cold kitchen tiles to the cupboard under the sink where the dog stuff is kept. I grab the packet of liver treats and tiptoe back to Bando in the lounge room. His tail whirls like a helicopter blade.

'Good boy. Staaayyy.' I think I hear a noise. I listen for Mum. I do not breathe for thirty seconds or more before I decide that it was nothing.

I slide the ugly bowl to the corner of the

chest of drawers. I make a show of sprinkling the treats inside. Bando watches carefully. A long thread of saliva droops from his mouth onto the floorboards.

'Staaaayyy,' I whisper. I move the bowl to the very corner of the chest of drawers, and I step back slowly towards my escape route.

'Okay . . . Go!' I whisper sharply.

Bando runs on the spot, Scooby-Doo style, his claws desperately trying to grip the slippery floor. He finds his footing and gallops towards the bowl, skidding to a stop and bumping into the drawers. They are too high for him.

He reaches up to put his paws on the edge. He bumps the bowl, just as I had planned.

This is Bando within a country mile of liver treats.

It starts to fall, slo-mo, towards the ground.
It spins and twists through the air. I begin to
worry that the bowl might not break, but,
in that instant, gravity does its thing and –
bam! – it hits the floor, exploding, sending
pieces flying everywhere. Millions of them.
Under the couch, onto the rug, even into the
kitchen. Bando starts to devour the treats.

My body zings with the thrill of the crime,
and I feel an urge to sprinkle liver treats into
some of the other ugly ornaments around the
house. I want to fill the heads of my sister's
creepy porcelain dolls with them. I want to
scatter them through her socks and undies
basket where she keeps her diary.

But I don't.

I drop the bag of treats into a drawer,
gently close it and tiptoe across the lounge

room, down the hall and into my room, careful not to tread on any jagged pieces of bowl. I ease myself onto the bed and shove my headphones in like I've been listening to music the whole time.

I. Am. A genius.

Life will be better for me after this. Bando will start taking some of the heat, and I won't have to spend the rest of my childhood wishing I was a dog.

I wait.

I listen.

I wait some more.

I do not hear footsteps.

I take out one of my headphone earbuds.

Nothing.

Tanya, my sister, is at swimming, but Mum should have heard it.

I tiptoe across to the door of my room and peek down the hall.

Bando is still scouring the wreckage of the bowl, sniffing madly for more treats. I glide up to Mum's bedroom door, open it a few centimetres and peer in.

Asleep.

How could she be asleep? It sounded like a bomb exploding. What does it take to make your mother angry around here?

I go to her bedside and see that she's wearing earplugs. Garbage bin day. She does this on Tuesday mornings so that she doesn't wake up at five-thirty.

'Mum,' I say quietly.

Nothing.

'Mum,' I say a little louder.

All I can hear is Bando sniffing and

tap-dancing around in the lounge room. It's really starting to get on my nerves.

I pluck out an earplug. 'MUM!'

She sits upright and says, 'Wha–, wha–', like she's woken from a nightmare. But, really, she has woken into one.

'Sorry,' I say. 'Bando. He knocked over your favourite bowl.'

'What?' she asks again.

'He kind of went mad and knocked into the drawers, and he just . . . smashed it. Come see.'

She groans loudly, puts on her slippers and follows me out.

'See?' I say, pointing to the scene of the crime.

'Oh, Tom, what happened?' she says.

Bando has disappeared, which is not helpful to my case.

'Well, he was just . . . he ran through and jumped up, and it just . . .'

'Why would he do that?' she asks, picking up a large piece of the horrible bowl and turning it over in her fingers.

'Like I said, he just kind of went mad. I guess he's getting old and weird,' I say.

She kneels down and picks up another piece, examining it closely.

'Maybe it was him who broke the laptop, too?' I suggest.

I am desperate...

Maybe it was Bando that held up that service station recently... and blew up that fireworks factory.

She glares at me and I know I've made my move too early.

'Where were you when this happened?' she demands.

'In my room.'

'Doing what?'

'Listening to music. With headphones on.'

'At this time of the morning?'

'Mm-hm.' I nod.

'And you didn't hear it?'

'Nope.'

'So how do you know it was Bando, and how do you know he just "ran through and jumped up"?' she asks.

'Well . . .' I say. How can she roll out of bed and be like a forensic scientist seconds later? I have to tread very carefully here.

'Because he was still here when I came

out,' I say, 'right in the middle of the wreckage.'

Bando comes to the lounge room doorway from the kitchen, panting loudly, smiling his goofy, black-lipped smile.

'Bad boy!' Mum says. 'Sit!'

Bando drops, rests his chin on the floor, looking guilty. I feel kind of bad. But only kind of.

'I think we should sell the dog,' Mum says, glaring at him.

I laugh. I know she's joking but it's still nice to hear.

'Go and get me the vacuum cleaner.'

'Yes, Mum.'

I head off down the hall, not skipping but close. I think she's buying the story, which means that, in one slick and cunning move,

I have framed Bando and destroyed the ugliest bowl in the history of ceramics. I wrestle the vacuum cleaner out of the cupboard and head back up the hall.

Mum is kneeling on the floorboards, scraping the pieces together with her hands. Tiny fragments fall into the cracks between the boards. I plunk the vacuum down next to her.

'Thanks,' she says quietly, sniffling.

'Are you okay?' I ask.

Bando gets up and snorts through the broken bits again.

Mum wipes her nose. 'I remember the man I bought this bowl from,' she says. 'A little old guy at the market in Marrakesh in Morocco when I was backpacking. Looked like he was a hundred years old. He made this for his wife who'd died, and he said that he wanted me to have it.'

'Really?' I ask. 'I thought you got it from a garage sale down the street.'

'He said my eyes reminded him of hers. Didn't even want me to pay for it, but I did. Can you plug this in?' She hands me the cord and I drag it across the lounge room to the power point. I can feel a little lump in my throat. I didn't know any of this.

Bando is sniffing around the drawers where I put the treats.

'Bando! Outside!' I plug the power cord in.

'Tom . . . What's this?' Mum says. She picks up a small, dark-brown piece from the floor and inspects it. 'This doesn't look like my bowl.'

'Huh?'

She pokes her finger at a gooey residue on the piece and rubs her fingers together. 'Saliva.' She sniffs it. 'It smells like tuna.' She sniffs again. 'No, more like . . . liver.'

I swallow so hard I almost swallow my lips.

'Why on earth would there be a liver treat in among the broken pieces of my bowl?' she asks, turning to me.

Bando is really sniffing that drawer like mad now.

I shrug. 'I wasn't there. Maybe . . .'

'Show me your headphones.'

'What do you mean?'

'Show me.' She grabs my headphones out of my hand. She snaps on the lamp that sits on top of the drawers where the bowl once sat. She holds one of the earbuds up to the light.

'Hmm,' she says.

'What?'

'Interesting.'

I can feel the heat of the lamp. I undo the top button of my pyjamas. It feels kind of warm in here.

She wipes her pointer finger over the earbud and then studies her fingertip, close to the naked bulb of the lamp. She almost looks professional.

Since when did MUM get her detective licence?!

Even with my top button undone I'm burning up. I wipe away the sweat trickling down my temple.

Mum dusts her fingers on her dressing-gown and stands. I have never noticed how tall she is before. She towers over me. I can see right up her nostrils. They are wide and horse-like. She is an angry horse-detective.

'Did you have anything to do with this, Tom?' she asks, looking into my eyes.

Bando growls.

'No,' I say.

Her nostrils flare wider. 'There appear to be liver treats in among the broken pieces of my favourite bowl and trace elements of liver treat dust on your headphones. You seem to know detailed information about the breakage of the bowl, even though you were not in the room at the time. Your breathing is short and you have sweat running down your face.'

'But . . .'

She raises a finger and looks at me in a knowing way. 'I'm taking a walk through your mind right now, Tom Weekly, and I am sensing panic, confusion, a spiralling sense of fear . . . and a wish that you had never set this whole thing in motion. Am I correct?'

It seriously feels like she's walking down the dark corridors of my brain, shining a torch into places even I haven't seen.

'I'm going to ask you one more time, Thomas . . . Did you have anything to do with this?'

Bando growls again. He's pawing at the little brass handle on the drawer. It squeaks and knocks against the timber.

Mum twists the lamp just slightly so it shines in my eyes.

'TOM?'

That's it. I can't take it anymore. My head is about to explode. I only have one choice . . .

'NO!' I yell. 'It was him!' I point at Bando, the evil yet cute Labrador.

Bando barks and scratches the drawer with his claws. Mum rips it open, reaches in and pulls out the open bag of liver treats.

'Why are these treats in this drawer and not in the kitchen, Tom Weekly?'

'Would you believe Bando put them in there?' I ask.

'You're grounded for two weeks. Clean this mess up.' Mum slams the drawer and heads off down the hall, leaving me and Bando staring at one another.

'Oh, by the way,' Mum says, poking her head back into the room. 'I made up the story about the Moroccan man and his wife. I was testing you and I'm very disappointed that you didn't admit to what you did. I bought the bowl at a garage sale at number seventeen.'

She disappears down the hall again.

I can't believe it. Outsmarted by a dog and conned by my own mother.

And she calls *me* dishonest.

Bando yawns excitedly and smiles his goofy, black-lipped smile, looking up at me as though he's my best buddy.

Like I said, I think I hate my dog. And I wish I was him.

THE LAST KISS

Stella Holling is after me. I am hiding behind
a tree – a very large gum tree over near the
bubblers on the top oval. I am scared. Stella
Holling is on the other side of the tree, and six
or seven kids are watching us. Every now and
then she makes a break and tries to catch me,
and if she catches me she will kiss me, and I do
not want that to happen.

Not again.

Stella Holling has been in love with me
since second grade. I'm not saying that to brag.

(Believe me, nobody would brag about that.) It's just a fact. Ask anyone. Back in Mrs Freedman's second-grade class I bent over to pick up a red pencil, and she kissed me on the cheek. Stella Holling, not Mrs Freedman.

Weird, I thought. *Let's hope that doesn't happen again.*

But it did.

Many, MANY times.

And now I'm on the run. Stella has just eaten a packet of strawberry jelly crystals. Dry. Out of the box. That makes it even worse. A thousand times worse. Stella goes cuckoo when she eats sugar.

'Get him, Stella!' a couple of girls from my class call out, giggling like chickens a few metres away. Stella dashes around the tree, catches me off guard and grabs the back of

Things I'd rather do than kiss Stella Holling

1. Lick the road.
2. Eat a stink bug (2 even!)
3. Wear my sister's perfume for a YEAR.
4. Tell Pop that I'm a Commie (whatever that is.)
5. Ride the school bus pretending that I didn't realise that MY underpants were on the outside.

my shirt. I panic and run, only just managing to escape. She chases me around the tree twelve times before she stops to catch her breath, and so do I, in the same places we started. She really means business today – she usually gives up after ten minutes. She has been chasing me all recess. I think she's been training for this.

'Pssst!'

I turn. Stella is leaning around the tree, where the kids watching us can't see. Her eyes are spinning from the jelly crystals and she is dripping with sweat. She speaks in a sharp, dangerous whisper. 'Either you kiss me on the lips now, Tom Weekly, or I want you to pay back every cent of the money you've borrowed from me.'

This sometimes happens when the sugar starts to wear off. Stella turns mean and tells me she hates me. I can't remember how much money she has given me. She has always offered it so freely. Whenever I'm hanging around the canteen looking hungry, which is a lot, she gives me her spare change to buy chips or an iceblock. I thought she was just being kind. What a fool. What a stupid, blind fool I have been.

'You owe me seven dollars thirty-five, in case you're wondering,' she whispers fiercely, then she runs at me, but I make it around the tree.

'Kiss him, Stella!' Jack calls out from the crowd of onlookers. That's what best friends are for, right?

'I can't kiss you,' I say in a low voice. 'You know that I like Sasha. And you gave me that money. You never said you wanted it back.'

'Sasha Schmasha,' she says. 'And I do want the money back. I'll tell Mum you *stole* the money from me. Bullied me. It's your word against mine.'

Stella's mum works in the school office and is pretty pally with the principal.

'You wouldn't do that,' I say.

She gives me her 'just try me' look.

This is bad. Stella is a dangerous person. Mad, bad and dangerous. How can she twist things like this?

Seven dollars thirty-five.

I try to remember how much I have at home, how much I have stashed in the hole at the base of the tree near the post office. But who am I kidding? I'd be lucky to have two dollars all-up.

'Made up your mind yet, you little baby?' she whispers.

'I'm thinking,' I say.

One little kiss. That's all it is. And the debt will be paid. Seven dollars thirty-five for one second's work. When I leave school and get a job, if someone offers me seven dollars thirty-five a second that will be, like . . . four hundred and forty-one dollars a minute or twenty-six thousand four hundred and sixty dollars an hour. That's over a million bucks a week.

One kiss and I'll be a millionaire! Sort of.

So I do it.

I hold up my hands in surrender, walk around the tree and stand next to Stella, who is grinning her head off.

'Whoo-hoo!' a few of the girls cheer. Jack claps. They watch on, excited, knowing what's coming.

Stella turns to me. She closes her eyes and smooshes out her lips. They look like a dangerous sea creature – something a small fish might find on a coral reef and think is safe but then – *sssssslp!* – gone. Never seen again. I wish I was kissing a crocodile. Or

Ms Trunchbull from *Matilda*. Or Jabba the Hutt. Someone or something less scary than Stella Holling.

The kids are chanting: 'Go! Go! Go! Go!'

Stella's lips
- patrolling the ocean
of my dreams

I have to get this over with. It's not like she hasn't kissed me a thousand times before. I lean forward. She leans forward. I can feel jets of air spewing from her nose. I can see her freckles in close-up. I can feel the warmth of her face. Our lips are almost touching. I can still back out. I can still run. I can . . .

But I don't.

I kiss her.

On the lips.

Stella Holling.

The kids go dead quiet.

The world stops spinning.

It's like we have fallen through a wormhole in space, where a second does not feel like a second. It feels like a week, a month, a year. Suddenly I am being paid 0.0000000000000003 cents an hour, rather than twenty-six thousand four hundred and sixty dollars. This is sweatshop labour. The United Nations should step in to stop this kiss. Nobody in the history of time has ever worked this hard for seven dollars and thirty-five cents. It is the longest and worst second of my life.

In my mind there is an explosion of colour,

like fireworks, and then a rapid-fire series of pictures: Stella and me cutting a wedding cake, Stella and me standing next to a 'For Sale' sign with a 'SOLD' sticker across it, Stella and me with two freaky-looking kids, Stella and me in a nursing home with sloppy food dripping down our chins. A twisted version of everything I have ever dreamed of for Sasha and me is happening with Stella instead. This kiss is rewriting my future. I can't handle it anymore, and I feel myself travelling backwards through the rainbow-coloured wormhole and then . . . *Pop!*

I leap away from Stella and wipe my mouth.

I feel older. Not like a teenager, but like I am eighty, like my entire life has been wasted on that kiss.

There is cheering. Lots of it. The girls and Jack point and laugh, but the cheering is much louder than that. I look over past the bubblers towards the school fence and I see them – about fifty boys from the high school across the street are lined up along the fence in their green-and-grey uniforms, clapping and whistling and shouting things that I probably shouldn't repeat. They have seen it all.

A voice rings out across the playground from the speakers attached to the side of the main building: 'Thomas Weekly and Stella Holling, report to the office immediately!' It's the principal's voice.

'Thomas Weekly and Stella Holling. There will be no kissing in the playground. I repeat, students are not permitted to kiss one another in the playground. Report to the office.'

The high-school boys go wild, and every kid in our playground who didn't see the kiss now starts howling and hooting.

I look to Stella, expecting her to be looking at me all misty-eyed after kissing the boy of her dreams. But, instead, she wipes her lips and scrapes at her jelly-crystal-stained tongue and says, 'That kiss was disgusting!'

Right in front of everybody.

The girls stop laughing and just kind of stare at me with pity. Maddie and Jessica put their arms around Stella and lead her to the bubblers, where she rinses her mouth, as though *I* am the crocodile or Trunchbull or Jabba the Hutt.

And you know what the worst part is? Sasha is standing there looking at me and shaking her head. It is worse than the fifty high-school boys, worse than the principal's office.

'It didn't mean anything!' I say, but she turns sharply and walks away.

'That was bad,' Jack says, coming up beside me. 'Stella burnt you so bad.'

'I know but –'

'You should move away.'

'Huh?'

'If you ever want to have a girlfriend, you should move away to, like, Venezuela or somewhere.'

'Where's Venezuela?' I ask.

'I don't know, but you should go there

because no girl is ever going to forget that
kiss.'

'But I . . .'

'Seriously, dude. Venezuela,' he says.

At lunchtime I'm all alone and I walk past the
canteen. I never want to eat another packet
of chips or another iceblock as long as I live.
Those things only lead to having to kiss girls,
and kissing girls only leads to trouble.

Stella Holling is standing in line. I look
away, walking faster, trying to escape before
she sees me.

'Tom!' she calls.

I glance back. I can't help it. She waves me
towards her. I want to ignore her, but I feel bad
about everything so I slink over.

'Sorry,' she says. 'It was the strawberry jelly crystals. They kind of make me –'

'I know,' I say. 'You really should stick to blueberry.'

We stand there for an awkward moment.

'Do you want some money for an iceblock?' she asks.

I look her in the eye. 'You're kidding, right?'

Stella shakes her head.

'You're the weirdest person I have ever met,' I say.

'I know.' She holds out seventy cents.

'I'm not kissing you again,' I say.

'As if I'd want you to,' she says.

Stella makes it to the front of the line and buys me an iceblock. She knows my flavour. I know I shouldn't eat it but it's lemonade, so I take the iceblock and bite into it. The cold, lemony goodness slides down my throat and washes away the horrors of the day. I feel better, and maybe I won't have to move away to Venezuela after all.

'You know what?' Stella says as we shuffle away from the canteen.

'What?'

'I was only kidding before.' And she gives me this weird look. 'The kiss wasn't really disgusting . . .'

Then she makes a face that scares me slightly. It's a look I've seen before, like a dangerous sea creature a small fish might find on a coral reef.

I drop the iceblock and run.

One ticket to as far away from Stella Holling as possible.

Acknowledgements

I would like to thank students at the following schools and events who helped me to write this book. I shared story ideas and we brainstormed renegade toddlers, dangerous backyard theme park rides, ways to frame a dog for a crime and despicable things that brothers and sisters do to one another. Thanks to year 8/9 writing students at Brisbane Girls' Grammar for introducing me to star-nosed moles. Thanks to Ipswich East SS year 5/6 kids, Calamvale Community College year 5/6/7s, Ascot SS, Brisbane Boys' Grammar middle-grade writing group, Sydney Writers' Festival Primary School Days participants 2012, Cowan and Brooklyn PS, Brookfield SS, Chatswood Hills SS, Roselea PS, Grace Lutheran, Kuraby SS year

6/7 writers group, Nobby SS, Greenmount SS, Our Lady of Mt Carmel Coorparoo, St Laurence's College, Berrinba East SS, Trinity Lutheran College, Marymount College, St Augustine's, Mullumbimby Library school holiday kids, Expanding Horizons Camp at Barambah, Tara Anglican School for Girls years 7 and 9, and the Bardon Young Writers Week participants 2013.

Extra-big thanks to Gus Gordon, Zoe Walton, Sophie Hamley, Brandon VanOver, Dot Tonkin and the booksellers, librarians and teachers who share my books with kids and tirelessly promote literacy. Cheers also to Raph Atkins for being an all-round funnyman and creative talent.

About the Author

Tristan Bancks is a children's and teen author with a background in acting and filmmaking. His books include the Tom Weekly series, Mac Slater series and crime-mystery novels for middle-graders, including *Two Wolves* (*On the Run* in the US) and *The Fall*. *Two Wolves* won Honour Book in the 2015 Children's Book Council of Australia Book of the Year Awards and was shortlisted for the Prime Minister's Literary Awards. It also won the YABBA and KOALA Children's Choice Awards. Tristan is a writer-ambassador for the literacy charity Room to Read. He is excited by the future of storytelling and inspiring others to create. Visit Tristan at tristanbancks.com

About the Illustrator

Gus Gordon has written and illustrated over 70 books for children. He writes books about motorbike-riding stunt chickens, dogs that live in trees, and singing on rooftops in New York. His picture book *Herman and Rosie* was a 2013 CBCA Honour Book. Gus loves speaking to kids about illustration, character design and the desire to control a wiggly line. Visit Gus at gusgordon.com

Room to Read®

About Room to Read

Tristan Bancks is a committed writer-ambassador for Room to Read, an innovative global non-profit that has impacted the lives of over ten million children in ten low-income countries through its Literacy and Girls' Education programs. Room to Read is changing children's lives in Bangladesh, Cambodia, India, Laos, Nepal, South Africa, Sri Lanka, Tanzania, Vietnam and Zambia – and you can help!

In 2012 Tristan started the Room to Read World Change Challenge in collaboration with Australian school children to build a school library in Siem Reap, Cambodia. Over the years since Tristan, his fellow writer-ambassadors and kids in both Australia and Hong Kong have raised $80,000 to buy 80,000 books for children in low-income countries.

For more information or to join this year's World Change Challenge, visit tristanbancks.com/p/change-world.html, and to find out more about Room to Read, visit roomtoread.org.